ECHO OF THE WAVES

VINAYAK ARALELIMATH

Made with ♥ on the Notion Press Platform
www.notionpress.com

To my parents

Contents

Acknowledgements *vii*

1. Chapter 1 1
2. Chapter 2 7
3. Chapter 3 13
4. Chapter 4 20
5. Chapter 5 24
6. Chapter 6 29
7. Chapter 7 34
8. Chapter 8 43
9. Chapter 9 51
10. Chapter 10 55
11. Chapter 11 59
12. Chapter 12 62
13. Chapter 13 64
14. Chapter 14 67
15. Chapter 15 74
16. Chapter 16 79
17. Chapter 17 84
18. Chapter 18 89
19. Chapter 19 95
20. Chapter 20 104
21. Chapter 21 110
22. Chapter 22 114

The Next Beginning 117

Acknowledgements

I want to thank my family for their support throughout this journey. A special thanks to Deeksha, for her meticulous editing, and Yashaswee for the beautiful cover design. I also appreciate my wife for her constant support.

In the stillness of the early morning, at around 3 a.m. I stood leaning against the wall outside my room, gazing at the hostel building. A blanket of silence had descended over the building, with only the faint hum of my room's light breaking the stillness. It was a telling reminder of the reality that most of my classmates had already left college after their final exams. Yet, here I was, one of the few left behind, grappling with the weight of academic backlog.

The night outside was as dark as my thoughts. no moon. no stars. Just a vast expanse of blackness that mirrored the uncertainty I felt. The subject of my pending exam, PULSE, loomed over me like an ominous cloud, casting a shadow over my hopes and dreams.

The question that kept gnawing at me was, "What if I can't clear this backlog today?" Anxiety had me in its icy grip. The future was a murky pond, and I was standing at its edge, unsure of what lay beneath. The looming prospect of not graduating this year was a bitter pill to swallow. It felt as though I was standing alone on a stage, my failures spotlighted for all to see. As the minutes ticked away, my thoughts took a detour towards the divine. I found myself begging God, my voice a mere whisper in the stillness of the night. "Please, help me pass this exam. If I don't, I'll be the one left behind. I won't graduate this year. Please, God, lend me your strength this time! I won't ask for anything else. Please, help me!"

In that moment of profound desperation, I felt the enormity of my situation. I was standing at a crossroads, the path I chose now would determine the course of my life. Would I be the protagonist of my own story or a mere spectator? Would I overcome my challenges or let them define me? The answers to these questions lay in the hands of destiny and the grueling hours that were to follow. The quiet hum of the light in my room was a constant reminder of the path that lay before me - a path that I had to walk alone. Whether I would emerge victorious or be left in the shadows of my failures was a question only time could answer.

The night grew colder, and a brisk wind stung my face, seeping through my clothes. I desperately rubbed my hands together to generate some warmth. Amidst the biting cold, I found myself sneezing. The first sneeze arrived, followed promptly by a second and a third. An unease settled over me, for some superstitions held that an odd number of sneezes predicted misfortune, suggesting that challenges lay ahead. My anxiety deepened because I longed for a fourth sneeze to break this ominous pattern.

Unfortunately, the fourth sneeze didn't come, no matter how hard I tried. I even attempted a strange trick by putting the cap of my pen into my nose. "Oh God, please," I whispered, and, in an attempt to ease my unease, I let out an unconventional "ahh-choooo-aaa-csee" sound.

Returning to my room, I found Sandy, Amar, Jeevan, and Karthik all sleeping on the floor. Looking at them, I yearned to be in their peaceful slumber. Jeevan and I had been roommates for four years, while Amar, Karthik, and Sandy lived in the room next door. We were close friends in college and everyone called us "Sandy's gang."

For the past three days, they've been staying with me, offering help and support. I've also been thinking about the other side of the situation. If I had passed the exam, I might have missed out on understanding what true friendship is all about. They are here, putting in more effort than I am, determined to help me conquer my academic hurdles.

I noticed a hefty white textbook on the table. It was my PULSE book, a book I hadn't opened until now. That book seemed tailored for Sandy, and he's the one who had taken it from my shelf. Until today, I had relied on some old notes and a small book with solutions to previous exam papers. I focused on preparing for the 40 marks I was confident about, concentrating on questions and theorems that were likely to appear. But deep down, I was trembling with fear about not passing the exam and facing disappointment again, I couldn't even imagine what would happen if I failed. I felt like I had no other option but to do my absolute best.

Sandy had plans for a grand party that night – it was our last day at college, marking the end of our teenage years filled with fun and excitement. Life was about to take on a new phase of responsibility and career pursuits, and we were all going our separate ways.

He wanted me to be in high spirits at the party, and for that to happen, my exams needed to go well. Sandy had put in a lot of effort, tirelessly solving numerous problems and teaching me. I couldn't help but feel incredibly fortunate to have such amazing friends in my life.

With the party in mind, I decided to take a short nap. I gently pushed Amar's leg aside and closed my eyes. As I drifted off to sleep, I could feel the fatigue weighing down on my eyelids.

ᑭᑭᑭ

"Vinay... Vinayyyyy... exam... exammmm," Jeevan suddenly yelled, jolting me from my slumber.

I groaned from my bed, still half-asleep. "What exam?" I mumbled.

"Stupid! It's the Pulse exam," Jeevan impatiently clarified.

Instantly, I felt a surge of anxiety flooded my senses. "What's the time?" I urgently asked.

"It's already 8 o'clock; You need to get ready quickly" Jeevan replied

I had hoped to review a lot of material before the exam, but it seemed too late now. A sense of disappointment welled up within me.

"Get ready soon. You must be there by 9 o'clock" Jeevan emphasized, his voice filled with urgency.

I hurried into the bathroom and shut the door behind me, feeling a wave of sickness wash over me. I was struggling to remember the material I had studied, and I was anxious about not having enough time for last-minute revision before the exam. I was getting really nervous and angry at myself.

I shouted to Jeevan from the bathroom, "Please get my pen and find my hall ticket. It should be somewhere around here." But there was no response, and I began to suspect that Jeevan had fallen asleep again. So, I called louder, "Jeevan! Jeevan!"

Finally, he said he would look for it. But when I came out of the bathroom, he was asleep. I got frustrated and pushed him, asking if he found my hall ticket.

He woke up and started searching, and I also looked through my books on the table. Amar, who was on the bed, told me to check my pockets first, but it wasn't there.

Amar and Jeevan both joined in the search for my hall ticket. While I was getting dressed, I realized my belt was missing, so we began looking for that too.

"What are you guys looking for?" Sandy asked from his bed.

"I can't find my belt," I said.

Sandy teased, "Why do you need a belt for an exam? Someone get him some cream and powder. He's going to a beauty contest..."

I explained, "It's not about looks; it's my lucky belt."

"OHH OHHHH!!!" everyone exclaimed loudly.

"That's why you got Mukta as your girlfriend, thanks to your lucky belt," Sandy joked.

I gave him an annoyed look.

"Lucky belt," he repeated, this time differently, and everyone followed, saying, "Lucky belt."

Jeevan added, "He also lost his hall ticket."

Sandy turned to me, asking, "When are you going to get better, man?"

I replied, "I won't get better, what's your issue?"

"I think my bag has the hall ticket," I remembered suddenly.

"Wait a minute; you came to my room after the last exam... I think it's in my room," Karthik exclaimed and then rushed to his room.

He returned with my bag, and thankfully, my hall ticket and belt were inside. It was almost 8:30. Sandy started lighting his cigarette.

I scolded him, "I've told you a thousand times not to smoke in my room. I have allergies, man!"

"Okay, this is the thousand and one time, and you're going to the exam," he replied, glancing at Karthik.

Everyone wished me "All the Best!!"

As I was about to leave my room, Sandy said, "Wait, write with this pen."

"Lucky Pen, huh?" I remarked with a different tone.

Everyone joined in, saying, "Lucky Penaaaaaa."

"I don't want my effort to go to waste..." Sandy said.

"I know I'm dumb" I admitted.

"You're not dumb. We're dumb to have you as a friend..." Sandy and I started bickering again. Jeevan stepped in and said, "Go, it's time..."

I walked down to the college campus and entered the exam hall.

At 12 o'clock, I walked out of the exam hall and made my way to the college's main gate. I noticed our gang had gathered near the "pan shop" across the road from the college campus. Sandy was smoking, and the others were sitting on the campus wall

As I approached, I kept my head down, and they could tell from my demeanor that the exam hadn't gone well. Amar came over to the road and asked, "What happened? How did it go?"

I didn't reply. I went straight to Sandy and demanded, "Give me a cigarette," trying to snatch it from his hand.

Sandy questioned, "Why, man? This isn't your room."

"I need to smoke, just give it to me," I was getting really frustrated.

"You forgot... you have an allergy, right?" Sandy reminded me

"Today is just not my day," I muttered, continuing to try and grab the cigarette from his hand.

"It's okay. If the exam didn't go well, we'll come with you next time too. Don't worry," Sandy reassured, raising his hand.

"Alright, I'll buy a new cigarette," I said, starting to head towards the pan shop.

Karthik rushed towards Sandy and snatched the cigarette from Sandy's hand, urging me to take it, "Here, take it, take it..."

Jeevan came and took the question paper from my pocket, and he and Amar started looking at it.

"Damn! It's easy, buddy... the same problems we revised yesterday," Amar exclaimed to me.

I took a puff of my cigarette while sitting on a wall, but when the smoke entered my lungs, I started coughing and couldn't control my laughter. I laughed and coughed at the same time.

Amar pushed me off the wall, and everyone rushed over, they playfully began to hit me while laughing.

"Sorry... Sorry," I managed to say.

"I'm starving... Let's go have a good lunch. How about going to the Punjabi dhaba?" Karthik suggested, looking at everyone's faces.

"I haven't had anything today, except for that one sip of cigarette... I want to grab something at the college canteen first. Then we can go where you like," I said.

Sandy suddenly remembered his cigarette, and he began searching for it where I had fallen. It was still there, still lit. Sandy picked it up.

"Why are you taking that one? Just get a new one," Amar suggested to Sandy.

Sandy replied, "I'm not as rich as you."

"Okay, you want a cigarette take it take it" Sandy came over to me, trying to force it on me.

"You are giving us a shock... okay, wait, we'll give you a thousand-volt shock tonight, just wait and watch," Sandy teased.

"What's this shocking news?" I asked.

"Wait and watch," Jeevan replied cryptically.

I knew they were just teasing me, so I decided to play along. "Is this news related to Mukta?" I inquired.

Sandy chuckled, "You always come back to Mukta, don't you?"

"I'm just asking," I said.

"We're not entirely sure what it's about, but it might have some connection to your dear Mukta," Jeevan added cryptically.

We started walking toward the college canteen.

"What will you do if you never see her again?" Sandy asked me.

"Why wouldn't I see her again?" I wondered.

"We're all going home tomorrow. Are you not going? College days are over... Open your eyes, grow up. Your mother and your family are waiting for you. Mukta is not your family..." Sandy said sternly.

I felt embarrassed for asking such a foolish question to this guy. "I've never even talked to her; you guys are unnecessarily linking my name to hers..." I shouted at him.

Sandy retorted, "Oh, it's unnecessary... We thought it was a necessary connection," with a slightly different tone.

"Why do you always seem to target me?" I questioned Sandy.

"I've never done that... I've always stood where there is truth," Sandy replied.

"So, you mean I'm lying?"

"I never said that..."

"But it means the same thing, doesn't it?" I inquired.

"I don't know, that's up to your interpretation," he remained steadfast. I was seething inside.

Karthik and I went to wash our hands in the canteen.

I was eager to share some hot news with Karthik, but I also wanted to inquire about the shocking news.

"What's this shocking news everyone's talking about?" I inquired Karthik.

"Everyone's just teasing you... it's nothing," he shook his head.

"I met Murali in the exam hall, and he told me some juicy news," I said.

"What is it?" Karthik asked.

"Mithun proposed to Mukta on the last day of our exams it seems" I shared.

"Oh, is that so?" Karthik's expression changed.

"Don't tell Sandy about this. He unnecessarily bothers me," I requested.

"Everyone already knows about it... we didn't want this news to disturb your exam" Karthik explained.

I looked at Karthik, and he put his hand on my shoulder, saying, "Stay calm."

"You're also starting to sound like Sandy," I remarked, and we shared a laugh. We returned to our table, wiping our hands with handkerchiefs. The only edible option in the canteen was Pulav, and that's what we always had when we came here. We didn't bother looking at other choices.

Suddenly, Karthik said, "The shocking news is no longer shocking."

I stared at him.

Sandy understood. He's quite sharp, I realized.

"Looser," Sandy said with a tad different tone looking at me.

Suddenly, everyone chanted in unison, "Loser, loser," each rendering the word with their unique tone and pitch.

"Did I propose to her? Why you people are calling me a loser? Not even I looked at her! Why are you associating my name with her" I shouted.

I know I can never beat Sandy in any argument. He always proves he is right

"Who went with her to the college library? Who gave her a lift on a bike to her house? It is okay; you did these things as a friend but you never shared any of it with your best friends who are with you 24/7. We had to hear it from someone else. That's not fair," Sandy shouted at me.

"I agree that, but I did not tell you people all about this because you people pull my leg and make fun of me. I never went and asked her 'I will give you a drop to your house'. She only came and asked me when I was standing at a bus stop, what could I do?" I yelled

"You know why she asked you on that day?" Sandy asked me

"How I know man, she told some urgency that's all"

"Did you ask her, what urgency?" Jeevan asked

"She got periods or what?" Sandy laughed.

I got angry "How do I know, why she asked? what urgency she had?, if you people want then go and ask her. Why you are troubling me? I will go. Enough is enough. I pushed my chair back and started going towards the door

Amar and Karthik pulled me back; again, I sat on the chair with my face down.

"You know one thing. We are saving you. We all know why she came with you... you dumb don't understand the logic of the mind game she played with you". Sandy shouted at me

"What game she played? She just asked me to drop" I shouted back

arre, Get some water for this guy. See, when she asked you, Mithun was also at the bus stop. They'd been hanging out together quite a bit, even going on motorcycle rides. On that particular day, she wanted to prove to Mithun that she had other admirers and make him feel a little jealous. She used you to get Mithun.

"Do you understand the consequences of your casual ride with her? Look at the other side of it. Mithun and his gang were waiting for your return. Luckily, I found out and went to Mithun. I explained that you were innocent. If I hadn't been there, you might have lost some body parts. got it? You're getting angry at me, the one who saved you. Dumb!! Can't you understand now?" Sandy yelled at me.

"I thought she was an innocent girl. I had no idea about all this," I replied.

"We also don't want you to know about all this until you finished your exams," Sandy said, looking straight at me.

"Mithun warned you before, right?" he continued.

"I didn't know he was at the bus stop," I mumbled, hanging my head down.

"Give me my pen," Sandy requested.

I handed it to him, and he got up, heading out.

"Sandy... Sandy..." I called after him.

"What?" he asked.

"Sorry," I said.

"No, I'm not running away. I'm just going to buy cigarettes. Wait, there are still many stories to tell..." he said.

"Okay," I resigned; feeling like my life would never go back to normal until I convinced him of my innocence. I was a little embarrassed.

"What other story?" I asked Karthik.

"Nothing, he just talks. Come on, let's go," Karthik replied.

"I'm not really in the mood for lunch," I said.

We all returned to the room.

3

I wanted to go back to my room and relax, trying to avoid Sandy. But Amar and Karthik insisted that I join them in their room, and Sandy followed.

Sandy asked, "Not coming for lunch?"

Amar said, "Vinay doesn't feel like it."

Sandy turned to me, "What's wrong?"

I stayed quiet, not wanting to speak.

Sandy asked again, "Come on, we're all leaving tomorrow. What's bothering you?"

I finally replied, "We wanted to hear a story, so we came to your room for that."

Sandy chuckled, "I think you have some girly genes in you... one day you might change gender"

Confused, I asked, "What do you mean? Your answer doesn't match my question."

Sandy remarked, "You always revolve around the same thing... that is girl's character. You can't seem to move on from it."

I retorted, "Alright, I have a 'girl character.' Tell me the story; it's the last day, and I want to hear."

Amar chimed in, asking, "What other story?"

Sandy took a seat on the bed and pointed at me, saying, "Remember, I'm not in your room."

"Don't smoke," I said raising my voice.

With a grin, he replied, "Then you can leave."

I conceded, "Alright, I'll adjust."

Sandy teased, "This adapting character is also like a girl, you know."

I played along, saying, "Okay, I'm a girl. Now, tell me the story."

"How low can you go? Are you changing your gender just to hear a story?" Sandy taunted with a different tone.

I remained silent, knowing it was futile to argue with him.

Everyone awaited Sandy's story, knowing that if he mentioned one, it had to be true; he never lied.

Sandy instructed, "Vinay, go stand next to Karthik and hold his right hand"

I questioned, "Why should I?"

He retorted, "Just do it. Stop showcasing your character."

"Amar, sit on Karthik's left side, and Jeevan, stand behind Karthik." Sandy instructed

Karthik asked in confusion, "Can someone tell me what's going on here?"

Sandy explained, "I'm taking a photo, don't worry."

Karthik inquired, "Where's the camera?"

"Just sit tight; I'll take the photo after the story."

"Okay, go on then!"

Sandy began, "Alright, here's the story. A few days ago, Parvati proposed to me..."

We all suddenly surrounded Karthik, as he was known for his peculiar reactions when angry. He typically threw whatever was nearby when upset. We were prepared to restrain him, as we knew he had feelings for Parvati, even though she had rejected him.

Karthik demanded, "What nonsense are you talking about? What was your response, Sandy?"

Sandy replied, "I told her I would ask my close friend Karthik and let her know..."

"He must have rejected her. You know him, don't you?" I said to Karthik

"Let's hear it from his own mouth..." Karthik insisted

Sandy explained, "I didn't want to hurt her feelings."

Karthik exclaimed, "What do you mean by that? Did you accept her proposal?"

"I never told that" Sandy said

"Alright, then what did you say?" Karthik asked

"Nothing," Sandy replied

"What do you mean by 'nothing'?" Karthik asked again

Sandy turned to Karthik and asked, "Do you remember those days when you were heartbroken, lying in bed for days, crying and creating a whole drama? Do you recall that time?"

I didn't understand why he was bringing this up.

Sandy raised his voice, "Think about all the efforts we made to get you back to life. Do you remember?"

Karthik looked surprised.

"If I had rejected her proposal outright, especially so close to the exams, can you imagine how she would have felt? Consider that. I'm not the only one involved; she had feelings for me too. If it weren't for the exams, I might have declined right away."

We were all wide-eyed in amazement.

I asked Sandy, "How did you know all of this? I never thought about it."

Sandy chuckled and said, "Smoke, smoke."

Karthik inquired, "So, you accepted her proposal just to save her from failing the exam?"

Sandy clarified, "You still don't get it. I told her I'd think about it and give her an answer after the exams."

"Did you give her an answer after the exams?" Karthik questioned.

"I have other life goals. I'm not ready to make any decisions now. I explained this to her, and she understood my point." Sandy replied

Karthik then asked, "What if she attempted something because of the love failure?"

"What can I do for that? Tell me. When she rejected you, she didn't even care," Sandy replied.

"Okay, what's your goal? Our goal was to get girlfriends, but we didn't succeed. You mentioned different life goals. What are they?" Jeevan asked.

"I don't know what my goal is," Sandy admitted.

Jeevan chimed in, "Hey Sandy, you've never shared any information about yourself with us. You know everything about us; this isn't fair."

Amar added humorously, "You've rejected two girls already—how lucky you are! Girls are the ones proposing to you."

Sandy responded, "It's not about gender; it's about the feelings and trust you have for someone. Look at Karthik; even though she rejected him, he still loves her."

Jeevan persisted, "Okay, tell us about your goals Sandy."

Sandy confessed, "I don't know."

Jeevan pressed further, "Then how did you tell Parvati that you have different goals?"

Sandy explained, "What I mean is that my goal in life is to become independent from myself."

Sandy's philosophical quest took us into the realm of profound introspection, where we grappled with the concept of becoming "independent from oneself." It was a notion that initially seemed enigmatic, leaving me with a sense of curiosity.

I probed Sandy further, seeking clarity: "Could you elaborate on what you mean by becoming 'independent from oneself'?"

Sandy continued on a metaphorical journey to explain his perspective: "Imagine life as a visit to a casino with $200 in hand. On the first day, fortune favors you, and you turn that $200 into $2000. you feel ecstatic like you're a genius, unbeatable. Yet, on the following day, as you return with those $2000, you lose it all. A wave of desolation washes over you, and you curse your own choices."

He continued, "Consider the emotions that accompany these experiences: joy in victory, misery in defeat. Where do these intense feelings of happiness or sadness originate? Are they intrinsic, emanating from within, or are they responses to external circumstances? If we probe deeply, we realize that these emotions are often stirred by external factors."

"These external entities, whether it's the casino or money, possess the remarkable ability to inject thoughts and feelings of happiness or sadness into our consciousness. In essence, they exert control over our mental landscape. In this scenario, can we genuinely define ourselves when our very existence is controlled by external things? We lose our core identity; our sense of self is submerged in relation to these external influences. My aspiration is to liberate myself from this external world," Sandy concluded, leaving us in contemplative silence.

We listened intently, not fully comprehending. I tried to grasp his meaning, saying, "Sandy, I think I understood two things from what you said. Either you win or lose at the casino, and when you lose, you shouldn't be sad, and when you win, you shouldn't be happy. You shouldn't feel anything. Is that what you mean?"

Sandy gently corrected, "Not precisely. What I intend to convey is that our lives are often dictated by external factors. We should strive to regain agency over ourselves, refusing to let external circumstances dominate us."

Puzzled, I inquired further, "How can we do that?"

Sandy turned to a metaphor involving a magnet, offering a tangible illustration: "Consider a magnet; it possesses an inherent character. When any metal object or another magnet approaches, it consistently exerts its magnetic force, drawing them closer. This unwavering behavior defines its essence. Even when a stone is brought near, the magnet remains steadfast in its character."

Jeevan, trying to grasp the concept, asked for another example. Sandy agreed and said, "Okay, let's use your example, Jeevan. I know what you look like. You have black hair and fair skin, and you wear spectacles. That's what I know about you. Now, imagine a world without mirrors. If you think about who you are, how would you recognize yourself? Try to conjure up a mental image of yourself."

We all began introspecting, trying to identify our own characteristics. After a minute, Jeevan responded, "I don't really know what I am."

Sandy continued, "Just like a magnet, you don't know your true character; you're influenced by external factors."

Jeevan, now curious, asked, "So, how can I discover my real character?"

Sandy responded, "I don't have all the answers, Jeevan. You need to find it for yourself without being swayed by external influences."

He went on to explain that desires, egoism, pride, greed, lust, and personal likes and dislikes often cloud our souls and make them impure. Such impure souls possess limited knowledge and power, limiting their potential.

Sandy emphasized that our bodies should aid our souls in attaining knowledge of the imperishable. If our bodies don't understand their purpose, how can our souls reach the Supreme Soul?

Sandy then closed his eyes, entering a deep state of meditation. He looked like a spiritual guru to me. Most of his teachings went over my head, leaving Jeevan somewhat contemplative, and Amar and Karthik lost in their own thoughts, likely searching for their inner characters.

Curious about Sandy's inner character, I asked him, "What do you think your inner character is?"

He responded, "I'm not sure; I have to search for it. But I can't live without cigarettes. They've taken control of my body, and there's no real Sandy without cigarette" he admitted.

Puzzled, I asked, "You're aware of this, so why can't you quit smoking?"

With a mischievous smile, he replied, "I enjoy troubling you."

I scolded him, saying, "Don't smoke now!" But he lit another cigarette without a care.

I sighed and remarked, "You share all this wisdom with others, but you don't follow it yourself."

He shrugged and said, "Maybe that's my inner character."

I couldn't help but whisper to myself, "What's the use of such a character?"

I felt a sense of relief as my college days officially came to an end, marking the conclusion of years of study. It was like a significant pause, after, life had moved so swiftly over the past four years. I used to be puzzled when people mentioned pursuing higher degrees. I'd think, "The sky provides rain, and the earth yields food. What's the need for more degrees?" I questioned why people made life seem so complicated and what they truly achieved in the end. Of course, this was just my personal viewpoint

On the evening of our last day in college, we went to a party. We were all set to depart the next morning, uncertain about Sandy's plans. Over the past four years, he had never spoken about his family or his home. He would visit one of our houses during each semester break but never shared any personal information. I knew that Sandy had taken the GRE, and he was waiting for the results. Others were planning to join MTech coaching classes, but for me, completing one degree itself was a significant achievement. I was planning to head to Bangalore to search for a job.

That night, we had a grand party. We shouted and laughed on the empty streets, ran, had playful fights, pushed and pulled each other, beat our chests, whistled, cheered, hugged, and jumped around on the deserted road for a long time. It was a perfect way to bid farewell to our college days.

Around midnight, we gathered under a massive tree by the roadside. Jeevan and Amar were almost out of control and lay down under the tree. I noticed that Sandy was weeping, and I raised an eyebrow in surprise. I wondered why the usually strong-willed Sandy was crying. I nudged Karthik and raised my eyebrows in Sandy's direction. Karthik looked at Sandy and asked, "Hey, what happened?" in a concerned voice.

Sandy quickly wiped his eyes with his palms and replied, "Nothing."

I couldn't resist making a sarcastic remark and asked, "Why is the eagle shedding tears today?"

Sandy replied with a laugh, "Because today, the squirrel came out of its tree nest." Hearing this, Karthik and I also burst into laughter. The three of us hugged tightly and shed some tears. I had a feeling that Sandy would leave without saying goodbye tomorrow morning. After spending four years together, I had become adept at predicting some of Sandy's actions, and I was determined not to let him go.

When we returned to the hostel, I couldn't sleep all night. I listened intently for any sounds from Sandy's room, ready to wake up at a moment's notice. As I had anticipated, Sandy began to pack his bags early in the morning, preparing to leave without telling us. I heard the door open and rushed to the corridor. Sandy was taken aback when he saw me waiting outside.

"Where are you going?" I asked.

Sandy remained silent, his face downcast, struggling to find the words. Tears welled up in his eyes, something I had never seen before. Unable to control my own tears, I hugged him tightly and whispered in his ear, "You're coming with me."

"Don't get in my way," he replied, laughing.

"Are you out of your mind? Where will you go?"

"Mind your own business," he chuckled.

"Sandy, please," I pleaded.

He pointed towards his table in the room. "I've written my address on that white paper,".

"Wait, I will check," I replied and entered the room.

To my surprise, Sandy locked the door from the outside.

"Sandy, don't do this!" I screamed from inside the room.

Ignoring my pleas, Sandy rushed downstairs with his bag. I quickly checked the white paper on the table, but there was no address written on it. Instead, I found a diagram - a Swastik symbol with a star image embedded on top.

I couldn't comprehend the meaning of this symbol. I went back to the door and began pounding on it, trying to get Sandy's attention. Jeevan woke up, puzzled by the commotion.

Sandy had disappeared, leaving us bewildered. Jeevan and I continued to pound on the door, and soon Amar and Karthik, who were in the next room, came out and opened the door, but Sandy was nowhere to be seen. It felt like he had vanished into thin air, like something out of a movie.

We returned to the room, still baffled by Sandy's actions. All that was left behind was the symbol - a star atop a Swastik.

"Sandy said this is his address," I said, but none of us knew how to decipher it.

I recalled something Sandy had mentioned about the Swastika once, saying, "The Swastika is a holy symbol, and the four segments represent different living beings - humans, celestial beings, fish, birds, animals, and those in hell," Jeevan reminded us.

"Then it must be related to the family concept he used to talk about," I replied.

Everyone nodded in agreement.

With heavy hearts, we bid farewell to the hostel and each other, taking our respective buses back to our homes. I couldn't help but stare at the symbol Sandy had left behind. It felt like I could see Sandy's face in it, and a flood of old memories, emotions, and long-buried feelings washed over me as I sat in my bus seat, reminiscing about the events of the past four years

5

Four years ago, I arrived at this college, and my first day there is still etched in my memory. My father accompanied me, and I was filled with apprehension about the possibility of ragging. Hailing from a different city, I didn't know a soul here, and this marked the first time I would be living away from home.

My initial impression of the college and hostel wasn't particularly great. The college was situated quite far from the city, and we reached the college campus via a local bus. We got off at the college entrance from the city bus, and a long driveway led from the entrance gate to the hostel building. On the right side, there was a playground surrounded by trees. The hostel building was quite old, with its walls painted in a faded pale blue color

My hostel room was labeled 101, and at that moment, I was the only occupant. I felt all alone and asked my father to stay with me for the night. The next day would mark my first day at college.

The following morning, we woke up early, took our baths, and headed to the college canteen for breakfast. Many other boys and girls, accompanied by their parents, were already present. All the faces were unfamiliar. After breakfast, my father left for home. I kept my eyes fixed on his retreating figure until it disappeared. I had the urge to throw my notebook aside and run after him, but I knew life didn't work that way. I simply kicked the ground lightly and walked toward the classroom.

Upon entering the classroom, I noticed it was quite large. I decided to sit in the middle of a bench, hoping to blend in with the crowd. The first class of the day was engineering mathematics, and the professor requested each student to introduce themselves before starting the session. My anxiety levels began to rise. One by one, students from the front row got up and introduced themselves. Sitting beside me was a boy named Sandeep Kumar.

When it was my turn, fear gripped me, and I even forgot my own name. I stood there, desperately trying to recall my name, while everyone in the class waited in silence. It was so quiet you could hear a pin drop. The math professor asked, "Your name, please?" I was completely blank. Sandeep Kumar, the guy sitting next to me, opened my notebook and whispered, "Vinay," while subtly tilting his head towards me. Suddenly, my name came back to me, and I managed to say, "Vinay," to the professor before quickly taking my seat.

After all the students had finished their introductions, the math professor immediately began the lesson. The boy sitting next to me, Sandeep Kumar, started bombarding the professor with numerous questions about the subject, and even the other students couldn't keep up with what the professor was teaching. Each time he asked a question, everyone in the class would turn to look at our bench, and even the math professor started directing his teaching toward us. I couldn't help but curse myself for choosing this particular bench. I decided that before the second period began, I would find a way to change seats. The math class had turned into an impromptu question-and-answer session between the professor and Sandeep Kumar, while the rest of us were merely spectators.

In an attempt to express my gratitude for helping me remember my name, I smiled at Sandeep Kumar, but he didn't return the smile.

Then I said, "Hi, Sandeep Kumar."

He pretended not to hear me.

"Hi, Sandeep Kumar," I repeated, this time a bit louder.

He turned around and looked around as if searching for something. Then he asked, "Are you talking to me?"

I was a bit confused. "Your name is Sandeep, right?" I asked.

"Oh, that's only for attendance. Call me Sandy," he replied.

"Okay. Are you staying in the hostel?" I inquired.

"Yes, my room number is 102." He spoke

"Is it? Mine is 101," I replied.

"Oh, we're neighbors." He exclaimed

I felt relieved to have a brilliant student living next door. I thought that if I went back to the hostel with this guy, he could help me deal with any potential ragging. So, I decided not to change my bench, and stay where I was.

The next period began, and once again, Sandy began bombarding the teacher with numerous questions. He asked about various aspects of the subject, leaving the rest of us, including me, amazed at how much he knew about the subject matter.

It seemed like the professor was becoming irritated with Sandy's questions. Just before the period ended, the professor inquired, "What was your percentage in your 12th-grade exams?"

Sandy confidently replied, "97."

The entire class was taken aback by this response, their eyes widening in surprise. The professor chuckled and asked, "How did you miss those 3 percentage points?" Laughter filled the classroom.

The professor then asked another question, "Why did you choose this college when there are so many better ones available?"

Sandy stood up, seemingly taken aback by the question. After a moment of silence, he finally answered, "Because of him. He is my best friend, and I wanted to be with him," as he placed his hand on my shoulder.

I was left feeling bewildered and shaken by his unexpected response. I couldn't understand why he had said that.

Suddenly, all eyes in the classroom turned to me, and the professor asked, "What was your percentage?"

I had no choice but to respond truthfully, "58 percent."

"Good combination," the professor remarked before leaving the class.

Laughter erupted in the classroom once again. I felt humiliated and berated myself for choosing the bench that had led to this embarrassment.

As the class ended, I waited for Sandy so we could head back to the hostel together. I was anxious about the possibility of facing ragging. Many students from our class wanted to befriend Sandy, and he was quickly surrounded by them.

I positioned myself near the door, anticipating his arrival. Time seemed to stretch as Sandy engaged in a conversation with his newfound friends. When Sandy concluded his discussion, he walked past me without even a single glance in my direction. My frustration grew, and I questioned what kind of person he was. Eventually, I decided to follow him.

"Sandy! Sandy!" I called out.

He turned to me and asked, "Do you need something?"

"I thought I'd go to the hostel with you since my room is next to yours," I replied.

"What's your room number?" he inquired.

"101," I responded.

"I'm not going to the room right now. I'm heading out. Do you want to join me?" he asked.

"Where are we going?" I inquired.

"Smoking...! Do you smoke?" he asked.

"No," I shook my head.

I reluctantly joined him, and he led me to the other side of the road, where there was a pan shop. I noticed that several seniors were already gathered there. Fear started to creep in; I knew that seniors often subjected juniors to ragging in such places. If I continued to follow Sandy, I would likely be in trouble. I considered leaving him and making friends with others who were more like me.

He went to the shop without a trace of fear, bought cigarettes, and returned to me. He started smoking without saying a word, and I watched his calm demeanor. I didn't dare to speak, eager to leave the place as soon as possible and avoid the seniors.

After Sandy finished his cigarette, we returned to our room without uttering a word to each other.

6

I had initially decided not to have dinner, as I had heard that seniors often caught freshers during dinner time in the hostel. My mother had packed some food items in my suitcase, so I planned to have those and go to sleep. No one had joined my room yet, and I was alone. I hoped that someone from the Electronics and Communication (E&C) department would become my roommate so that I could distance myself from Sandy's friendship.

Around 8 o'clock, my room bell started ringing, and fear gripped me. I wondered who it could be this time. Slowly, I opened the door, and to my surprise, it was Sandy.

"Are you coming for dinner?" he asked.

He was dressed in nightwear, wearing Bermuda shorts, a T-shirt, and flip-flops. I contemplated saying no but ended up nodding my head in agreement. I followed him, cursing myself for agreeing to join him. Sandy was a moody guy and wasn't talking to me like a friend. We entered the canteen, which was bustling with students. I was fine with the crowd because it allowed me to blend in. We finished our dinner without any incidents, and I was relieved that nothing had happened in the canteen, and no seniors had noticed us.

While passing through the ground floor, we reached a room with a large crowd. Many seniors were gathered there, and it was room number 50. Sandy was curious to see what was happening and kept looking at the room as we passed by. However, I kept my head down and walked fast without glancing at the commotion. I knew that some seniors must be ragging juniors in that room. As we crossed room number 58 and reached 59, someone called out to us from behind. My worst fear was realized as they took us into a room where some juniors were running around, performing a left-right march and addressing every senior with a loud "SIR." I was extremely tense, and Sandy went ahead to stand in front of some seniors who were sitting on cots. They asked for our names, and I replied as Vinay while Sandy introduced himself as Sandeep Kumar.

The seniors instructed Sandy and me to march quickly in attention, puffing out our chests, and salute every senior while loudly saying "SIR." I complied, marching like the other juniors and addressing each senior with a loud "SIR." Sandy, on the other hand, stood there lost in thought, not bothering to participate.

One senior angrily called out to Sandy, "Hey, Sandeep Kumar, don't you understand what we said?"

Sandy began to look around in various directions, perplexing everyone.

"What are you searching for?" asked another senior.

"I'm searching for Sandeep Kumar," Sandy replied innocently.

"What is your name?" one guy yelled at him.

"Sandeep Kumar" Sandy replied.

"Then why are you searching?" the senior questioned.

"Oh! You're calling me. Call me Sandy," Sandy clarified.

"Ohhhhhhh!!!! This guy is like a Bollywood character. From which movie did you learn this drama?" another senior asked, coming forward and holding Sandy's face.

Sandy remained silent, and I felt frustration building within me. I couldn't understand why he was inviting trouble and getting me involved.

"Hey, Bollywood Sandy, can you march fast now?" another guy inquired sarcastically.

As Sandy marched, his flip-flops made a loud chap chap chap sound...

I wasn't sure if Sandy was intentionally acting this way, but it was irritating not only me but also everyone else around, including the seniors. I kept wondering why he was behaving like this. I saw other students following instructions silently, and I wished Sandy would do the same.

Then, one guy yelled at Sandy, "Hey, remove your chappals and march!"

Sandy complied, taking off his chappals and continuing to march in the prescribed manner. To our surprise, some numbers were clearly written on the soles of his chappals.

One senior asked, "What is that number on your chappals?"

Sandy replied, "It's a phone number."

The senior exclaimed, "Hey, look, he's got a phone number written on his chappals!" He is seriously a Bollywood-type guy...

Everyone burst into laughter.

One guy, while asking, slapped Sandy on the face and said, "Whose number is this, Bollywood Shahrukh Khan?"

Sandy remained silent for a moment before answering, "It's the college principal's number."

Suddenly, the whole atmosphere turned tense, and everyone was shocked into silence.

"You're trying to scare us," one guy said as he slapped Sandy again.

Two more guys approached Sandy, and he remained calm despite the situation.

"We won't leave him. Let's call this number; he's acting too smart," one of them declared.

"Take him to the one-rupee coin booth near the canteen," another yelled.

They grabbed Sandy's shirt collar and began pulling him, and Sandy, with unwavering composure, followed their lead. A crowd gathered as news of the incident spread throughout the hostel.

Sandy approached the coin booth, placed one of his chappals on top of the coin box, and picked up the receiver. Everyone watched intently as he shouted, "Give me a one-rupee coin to insert; I don't have one."

One guy couldn't believe Sandy had asked for money and he angrily exclaimed, "How dare you ask us for money!" He struck Sandy hard, causing blood to flow from Sandy's nose.

I checked my pocket and found a coin, quickly running over to hand it to Sandy.

Sandy began dialing the number. After a few seconds, he spoke loudly into the receiver, "Ma'am, I want to talk to Principal Sir. My name is Sandeep Kumar."

A senior nervously mumbled, "This guy is serious; keep the phone, keep the phone," but Sandy paid no heed.

"Principal Sir, some seniors want to talk to you," Sandy said to the person on the other end of the line. A tense silence hung in the air.

"I don't know their names, Sir, but I'll give the receiver to them," Sandy continued, extending the receiver toward the seniors who had been involved.

Nervousness swept over everyone, and the seniors quickly scattered, trying to escape the situation.

"Hold on, Sir... Principal Sir wants to talk to you. Please, take the receiver," Sandy pointed out the guy who had hit him earlier.

"Wait, sir..."

"Okay, sir, I'll write it down."

"Principal, sir, want to provide one more number. Does anyone have a pen?" Sandy shouted, this time even louder.

A junior guy handed a pen to Sandy.

Sandy took off his other chappal and began writing.

"One... okay sir..., zero... okay sir..., zero... okay, sir. I'll call this number for any problems," he said with a raised voice and then hung up the phone.

"Principal sir asked me to call this number for any issues. Does anyone have one more one-rupee coin?" Sandy inquired.

In a flash, everyone started running away, leaving only a few juniors behind.

Sandy and I walked back to our room together. I said goodbye to Sandy before entering my room, but he didn't respond and didn't even look at me. Then, suddenly, he came back and handed me my one-rupee coin.

I was astonished. I had seen him insert it into the coin booth. How did he get it back? I wondered. Nevertheless, I was relieved that we wouldn't be bothered by seniors anymore. They had learned a lesson, and I silently chuckled to myself, reflecting on how quickly they had fled when trouble arose. I couldn't help but admire Sandy's courage; I was certain that he wouldn't run away from problems but would face them head-on. After this incident, Sandy became a hero in my eyes.

The following morning, a guy named Jeevan joined my room. Jeevan was fair and appeared to be a regular, not moody like Sandy.

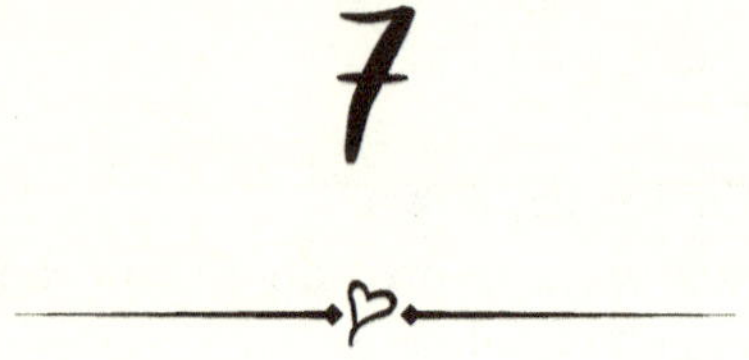

"Vinay told me that you taught a good lesson to the seniors yesterday," Jeevan said to Sandy.

Sandy responded, "What lesson?"

"You called the principal yesterday," Jeevan replied

"Yes, because of this guy, I was forced to call the principal," Sandy pointed at me.

I was shocked. "Why? What did I do?" I exclaimed.

"You gave me the one-rupee coin, didn't you?" he retorted

"You needed it to make the call, so I gave it to you," I shouted back.

"Not you, I asked those b******s..." he shouted back.

"They were hitting you, and to help you, I gave it," I explained.

"Who are you to save me?" he shouted

"What nonsense are you talking about? I'm your friend."

"But I'm not your friend. Don't interfere with my business..." Sandy replied, distancing himself.

"Are you mad?" I wanted to scream, but I couldn't find my voice. I just couldn't bear it. What had I done wrong? My heart started pounding, and I felt overwhelmed. Why did I join this college? Why did I meet this guy? My eyes filled with tears, but I held them back. I started walking towards the classroom, my thoughts a jumbled mess. Inside, I was crying, cursing, and sulking endlessly. It felt like my life had come to an abrupt end.

I took my seat in the middle of the bench, no one else in my row yet. Students started coming in, and I considered calling my home. I felt so alone, my heart still racing. After a while, Jeevan came and sat on my left side. I usually sat in the middle of the bench so that the professor wouldn't notice me.

Suddenly, Sandy came and sat on my right side. I didn't want to sit with him, so I considered changing my bench. However, the classroom was already filled, and the only vacant spot was in the front row. I didn't have the courage to go there, so I reluctantly stayed where I was. But Sandy seemed to be in a serious mood, and I felt it was best to keep my distance from him. I got up and moved to the front desk, which was the first time I had ever done so in a full class.

I sat on the front bench, feeling self-conscious, as if everyone in the class was watching me. I glanced left and right, but everyone was engrossed in their own activities, and I realized that my anxiety was unfounded. However, my heart was still pounding, and I couldn't shake the fear that if the professor asked a question and I couldn't answer, the whole class would laugh at me. I contemplated whether I should stay or leave the class.

As I was lost in my thoughts, the Mechanics professor appeared in front of me. Since this was his first class with us, he instructed us to introduce ourselves. My legs began to tremble as I stood up. I struggled to speak, and my voice was trembling. The anxiety was overwhelming, and I even forgot my own name. I felt lost and didn't know what to say. The professor stared at me, and I knew I had to respond to his simple question: "What is your name?"

I managed to stammer out my name, "Vinay," and the professor instructed me to sit down. As the students on the next bench began introducing themselves, I couldn't shake the feeling of humiliation and inadequacy. Even though nobody laughed or made fun of me, I felt deeply embarrassed and couldn't understand why I always seemed to struggle in such situations. My lack of confidence and courage weighed heavily on me.

Feeling utterly defeated and overwhelmed, I began to think that I was simply not cut out for college life. The embarrassment and frustration from the introduction incident lingered, and I contemplated returning home. During the Mechanics class, I struggled to comprehend the material, while Sandy continued to ask numerous questions to the professor. Each time I heard Sandy's voice, my frustration and irritation grew.

I eagerly awaited the end of the period, hoping to escape the classroom and skip the rest of the day's lectures, and perhaps even consider leaving the college altogether. However, just as the mechanics professor was finishing up, the math professor was waiting outside. I couldn't slip out. In the math class, the professor mentioned, "Attendance is mandatory, and it will count for 10 marks..." This only added to my anxiety and uncertainty about what to do next.

Despite my initial fears and uncertainties, I decided to stay in the class after the math period. As the day progressed, I slowly grew more accustomed to sitting on the first bench and listening to all the lectures.

After completing all my classes for the day, I began to experience a headache. I decided to go back to my room and rest. The fatigue and stress of the day had taken a toll on me, and I needed some time to recover.

When I woke up, I found Jeevan in the room, busy arranging his things. Despite my presence, he didn't acknowledge me or greet me with a simple "hi." It seemed like he was absorbed in his own activities and had no interest in engaging with me. My headache was still bothering me, adding to my discomfort and feelings of isolation.

I decided to go out for tea, hoping it would help ease my headache and my emotional distress. I took a Crocin tablet before leaving. Despite my discomfort, I didn't have dinner that day. Seeing Sandy and Jeevan quickly form a friendship made me feel even more isolated and hurt. It appeared that they had no intention of reaching out to me, further intensifying my feelings of loneliness and rejection.

The next morning, I woke up early, took a bath, and headed to the warden's office. It was around 6:30 a.m., and the cleaning lady was already at work. She asked me why I was there so early and informed me that the office warden would arrive at 8:30 a.m.

I didn't want to return to my room, so I decided to wait. At around 8:30 a.m., an office supervisor arrived. I mustered the courage to ask, "I want to change my room. What's the procedure?"

He replied, "There is no procedure for changing rooms. Once a room is allotted, it cannot be changed. If you want to stay, you'll have to remain there. Otherwise, you can leave the hostel, but we won't refund your money."

I felt disheartened and was about to leave then he inquired, "Which room do you want?"

A glimmer of hope lit up inside me, and I replied, "Any room, as long as it's not room 101 or 102."

He seemed surprised and said, "Any room? Usually, people request room changes to stay with their friends."

"Give me the last room, perhaps number 110," I said, hoping to stay as far away from Sandy as possible.

The supervisor responded, "It will cost money."

Money? I was taken aback. "How much?" I asked cautiously.

He replied slowly, "Five thousand rupees."

My hopes were completely dashed. I realized it might be better to leave this place altogether. I rushed to a public phone booth, called home, and my mother answered. "Why are you calling us at this time? You don't have classes today," she exclaimed.

Glancing at the time, which was almost 9, I replied, "Okay, I'll call you tonight," and hung up. Then, I hurried back to the classroom, which was nearly full, except for the first row.

As I entered the class, I noticed Jeevan and Sandy staring at me. There was another new guy sitting with them on their bench.

I didn't have many options, so I reluctantly took a seat in the first row. Surprisingly, I felt somewhat comfortable today, and the fear of sitting in the front row had diminished. I was able to concentrate on the lecturer. After the second period, there was a fifteen-minute break. During the break, I sat alone on my bench while everyone else in the class had made new friends and was engaged in conversations. Jeevan was busy talking to the new guy. It was frustrating, and I often wondered why I was like this, why I was so timid.

I observed many boys and girls surrounding Sandy, asking him questions about the lecture. He behaved so decently with them. I couldn't understand why he treated me differently, especially when we didn't know each other well. At that moment, I started to think something was wrong with my face or my personality.

I was anxiously waiting for the 15-minute break to end. It felt like an eternity. I endured the break in silence, lost in my thoughts.

I continued to sit on the first bench and attended all the classes for that day. Once the classes were over, I returned to my room, where I still didn't engage with my roommates.

I called my father that night, and they were eagerly awaiting my call. When they answered, they asked why I had called so early in the morning.

With a heavy heart and a trembling voice, I finally confessed, "I don't want to pursue engineering anymore. I want to come back home. I miss both of you so much here."

My parents were taken aback by this unexpected news. They pressed me for an explanation, wanting to understand what had led to this decision.

Feeling overwhelmed, I struggled to articulate my feelings. I simply repeated, "I miss you both so much," my voice quivering with emotion.

In response, my father assured me, "I'll be there tomorrow by the time you finish your classes." His words offered some comfort in that challenging moment.

I returned to my room that night, unable to eat anything. My mind was consumed with thoughts of what to tell my father. Should I admit that his son struggled to connect with people? Should I confess that my nature didn't align with this environment? The fear of being ridiculed by my peers, and labeled as a primary school boy if they saw my parents on campus, weighed heavily on my mind.

Unable to find sleep, I anxiously awaited the rising sun. At the crack of dawn, around 6 o'clock, I rushed to the STD

booth to call my home.
Fortunately, they hadn't left home yet, so they answered the phone. I urged them not to visit, insisting that I was fine. However, my father remained determined, saying they would come anyway. I then suggested meeting them at the bus stand, told them not to come to college and they agreed to wait for me there.

On the third day, I chose to sit on the first bench, even though many other benches were empty. I wanted to avoid seeing Sandy's face any longer. When the class ended, I rushed to the bus stand to meet my parents. They arrived around 3 o'clock. As soon as I saw my mother, I ran to her and hugged her tightly. I couldn't control my tears, and my parents also became emotional.

They took me to a nearby hotel, where they asked me to wash my face. They ordered a meal for me because I hadn't eaten properly in the last three days. I felt weak, almost on the verge of collapsing. I couldn't taste anything. My mind was consumed by my own turmoil.

After I had eaten, my father asked, "What happened, Vinay?"

I stared at my plate, struggling to find the words. Finally, I whispered, "I don't want to stay away from you."

My parents exchanged a worried glance. They understood that this was more than just homesickness. It was a deep struggle within me, and they were concerned about my well-being. We continued to talk, and they tried to reassure me that things would get better with time.

My father spoke reassuringly, "Now you are not a small boy. Every weekend, we will come to visit you, so don't worry. Within 2-3 months, one semester will be completed, and we'll be there for you. We'll also call you daily to stay in touch."

My mother intervened, saying, "My son and I will stay here, renting a house. You do your job there and visit us every weekend. We have only one son, and I will not leave him like this."

I felt relieved that my mother had come up with a plan to be closer to me. It sounded like a good idea to escape from the hostel environment that had been causing me so much distress.

However, my father reminded us, "I've already paid for one year of hostel fees, which is not a small amount."

With tears in my eyes, I said, "I don't want to stay in the hostel, Papa."

My father asked if someone had been bothering me, but I assured him that no one had harassed me. I simply couldn't tolerate the hostel environment.

In the end, my father agreed to my mother's idea, but he made it clear that it wouldn't happen immediately. I would have to stay in the hostel for at least one more month while they searched for a house and made arrangements for us to move.

Then, I asked my father for 5000 rupees. He was surprised and asked why I needed the money. I explained, "I accidentally broke an expensive apparatus in the Chemistry lab."

They thought I had staged this whole drama because of the broken apparatus, and my father handed me the money, saying, "Don't worry about all these things. You could have told me about the accident over the phone."

My parents seemed somewhat relieved, thinking that my distress had been caused by getting scolded at college due to the broken apparatus.

I asked my father and mother to stay for one more day, and they agreed. We found a lodge to stay in, and that night felt like it should never end. I held onto my mother tightly, hoping that my breath would stop before morning. Despite putting on a smile, I was still filled with fear.

Somehow, I managed to fall asleep and forget everything. In the morning, my father woke me up, saying, "You're getting late for college."

I went straight to the hostel office, searching for the office supervisor to request a room change. However, he wasn't there initially, so I waited patiently.

Eventually, he arrived with a broomstick in hand.

Without wasting any time, he asked, "Have you brought the money?"

"Yes," I replied, handing over the 5000 rupees. I anxiously waited for his response.

"Shift to room 110," he instructed.

"Alright," I agreed, still awaiting further instructions.

"What are you waiting for?" he questioned.

"I need an allotment letter for room 110," I explained.

"No need for a letter; just go," he said and then headed back inside.

I trailed behind him and inquired if room 110 had already been allotted to someone else.

"I'll ask him to move your room 102. I'll handle it. Now go," he replied.

I couldn't help but feel irritated that he had taken 5000 rupees just to convey this message, but I was left with no other option.

I entered my room and noticed some cigarette butts scattered in front of it, confirming that Sandy had been there. Inside, Jeevan was still asleep. Without a word, I began packing my belongings, and I moved everything to room number 110.

I sat in room 110, which was still vacant, and no one had arrived yet. It was only 7:30 AM, and I had more than an hour left before college started, so I decided to rest for a bit.

Around 9 o'clock, I headed to college and took my usual seat on the first bench, just as I had been doing for the past four days.

After all the classes, when the bell rang, I began walking back to the hostel. As I was leaving, I heard someone calling my name.

I turned around and saw that it was Sandy who was calling me. I felt a sudden wave of fear, wondering why he was calling me. I didn't stop but continued to walk quickly, glancing back to see Sandy running after me. My anxiety grew, and I eventually stopped because I knew he wouldn't give up.

He caught up with me and casually asked, "We're going to the movies this evening. Do you want to join?"

I was surprised at how casually he could ask me this after everything that had happened.

"No, I have some work," I replied and started moving back towards the hostel.

Jeevan also arrived with a new guy, and Sandy instructed Jeevan, "Hey, take him to the canteen. I'll join you guys after I smoke," pointing at me.

Then Sandy moved towards the gate, and I also continued walking back to the hostel.

However, Jeevan yelled my name from behind once again, and I ignored him, hoping he would let me be. But he persisted, coming up to me and holding my hand, insisting that I join him for a moment at the canteen. I was hesitant and scared, not knowing what might happen next.

I asked Jeevan softly, "What is this all about? What do you guys want from me?"

He replied, "Are you joining us for the movie this evening?"

"No, I have to go now," I responded.

"Where?" he inquired.

"My parents are here; I need to see them off at the bus stop," I explained.

"Okay, just for 10 minutes. Sandy wants to talk to you for just 10 minutes," he pleaded.

I asked, "What does he want from me?"

"Don't be scared; he's a nice guy," Jeevan reassured me.

"I'm not scared," I insisted.

"Alright, do you want some tea?" he asked.

"No," I replied.

"Okay, I'll get one. By the way, this is Karthik," Jeevan introduced the new guy who had joined Sandy's room the previous day.

I greeted Karthik with a simple "Hi" as I sat in one of the canteen chairs. Jeevan and Karthik went to order tea, and I pondered whether this was my chance to escape. If Sandy were to show up, I had no idea what might transpire.

I quickly left the canteen and made my way towards the exit, carefully ensuring that Jeevan didn't notice me slipping away. As I descended the steps outside the canteen, I suddenly spotted Sandy approaching from the opposite direction. Panic surged through me, and I hastily turned around, reentering the canteen and taking a seat at the same chair.

I silently wished for Jeevan to return and sit beside me before Sandy entered. Fortunately, Jeevan and Karthik arrived first, taking seats on the opposite side of the table from me. Then, Sandy strode into the canteen, announcing loudly, "Hey Vinay, how are you?"

Everyone in the canteen turned their attention to Sandy as he entered and took a seat beside me. He seemed completely unfazed by the attention.

"How are you, man?" he asked, his voice friendly.

"Fine," I replied, my voice still trembling.

"Why are you so scared?" he inquired.

"Nothing, I'm fine," I stammered.

"That's common," he said, laughing. "He belongs to the Sciuridae family he is like squirrels, and I belong to the Accipitridae eagle family."

I didn't understand what Sandy meant by the "squirrel family" comment, and Jeevan asked for clarification.

"What is this 'squirrel family'?" Jeevan asked.

Sandy laughed and replied, "You belong to the ' Bovidae goat family'?"

Sandy then put his hand on my shoulder and asked me if I had noticed the change in myself over the past four days. I remained silent.

He continued, "On the first day, you were so scared, trying to hide yourself when the professor asked questions. Now, for the past four days, you've been sitting alone on the first bench. Have you ever thought about voluntarily sitting there? You're only doing it because you don't want to sit with me." He laughed again. "This is what I wanted from you."

Sandy went on to explain that he had intentionally created that conflict with me to help me overcome my insecurities. He didn't want me to rely on him as a friend or become dependent on him as a bodyguard. His intention was to make me more self-reliant.

I opened up my mind, realizing how I had been sitting confidently on the first bench without hiding or feeling scared. For the past 12 years of my school and college life, I had always chosen the middle bench and never dared to sit in the front row.

As I thought about this transformation, I couldn't control my tears. Sandy suddenly hugged me and whispered, "Don't worry, fear is common in the squirrel family, but you'll never see a single drop of tears in my eyes throughout my life. That's what being an eagle is all about."

"Thanks," I told Sandy.

"I have to go now; my parents are waiting for me," I explained.

As I started to leave, Sandy shouted from the table, "Shift your belongings back to your room."

I moved out of the canteen door, feeling relaxed. I went to the lodge where my parents were waiting.

They asked me why I was so late. I made up an excuse, saying I had an extra class.

Then I asked my father, "Pappa, what does the Squirrel family mean?"

"Squirrel family? Do you mean actual squirrels?" he replied.

"No, in humans, are there families like the Squirrel family and the Eagle family?" I clarified.

My father seemed puzzled and replied, "I've never heard of such families. Who told you about this? Are you okay?"

"It was my professor who mentioned it," I said.

"Well, we don't know about that. Since you've come here, you've been acting strangely," my father remarked.

I assured him, "Nothing, Pappa, don't worry. I'm fine now."

Then he shared some good news, "We found a nice house near your college, and we've already paid the advance."

I became angry and exclaimed, "Why did you pay without asking me first?"

My father explained, "You wanted to stay with us, and your mom will be moving here. I'll visit you weekly."

I had a change of heart and said, "That's all fine, Pappa, but that was yesterday. Today, I want to stay in the hostel."

My father was taken aback, asking, "What are you saying?"

I continued, "I don't want to stay in the house. How much did you pay in advance?"

"2000," my father replied.

I insisted, "Go and get it back. I want to stay in the hostel."

My mother exclaimed, "What's wrong with you?"

I apologized, saying, "Sorry, everything is fine at the college now. I've adjusted."

My father questioned, "What made you change your mind from yesterday to today?"

"I am Ok mama" I assured them,

"Okay, leave it. I'll get back the advance. don't change your mind again." My father said with a mix of concern and confusion.

I nodded my head in agreement. We went to the house owner, got our advance back, and then I dropped my parents off at the bus stop as they headed back to our hometown.

I had expected my father or mother to be emotional, maybe even shed some tears, because we were supposedly a part of the Squirrel family. However, they were firm, not showing any signs of worry, but they were clearly angry with me.

I couldn't make sense of this "new family funda" and wondered if it was another one of Sandy's tricks. I began to feel anxious and scared. I couldn't help but question whether I had made a mistake by canceling the house.

I was aware of how important that 5,000 rupees was for my father. He must have worked hard and saved for months to gather that amount. I decided that I needed to get those 5,000 rupees back. I was determined to shift my room again. So, I made my way to the hostel warden's room. He was sitting there, busy writing something.

I approached the hostel warden and mustered the courage to speak up. "Sir, I don't want to change my room; I need my money back," I said.

He remained silent, engrossed in his work, as if ignoring my plea. I waited for a while and then called out again, "Sir."

I knew this person hadn't even passed his 10th grade, yet we had to address him as "Sir." I called out once more, "Sir."

He suddenly raised his head, and his face contorted with anger. I was frightened, but I couldn't back down now.

He abruptly stood up, marched towards me, grabbed my shirt collar, and forcefully pushed me towards the door, expelling me from his room.

I couldn't contain my frustration, and I raised my voice, shouting, "I need my money!"

In response, the warden yelled at me, "Get lost"

Defiantly, I threatened, "I will report this to the principal!"

He retorted, "If you know his father, go tell him too, but don't ever show your face here again!" With that, he slammed the door shut, leaving me standing outside.

I returned to room 110 and sat down on my bed, feeling defeated and frustrated.

I was filled with regret and disappointment in myself. I knew I didn't have the courage to explain this situation to the principal. What reason could I give for wanting to change my room? It was just too embarrassing.

As for Sandy, I had my doubts about whether he would help me or just make fun of me. Guilt gnawed at me.

That night, I stayed in room 110, but the next day, I decided to shift back to room 102.

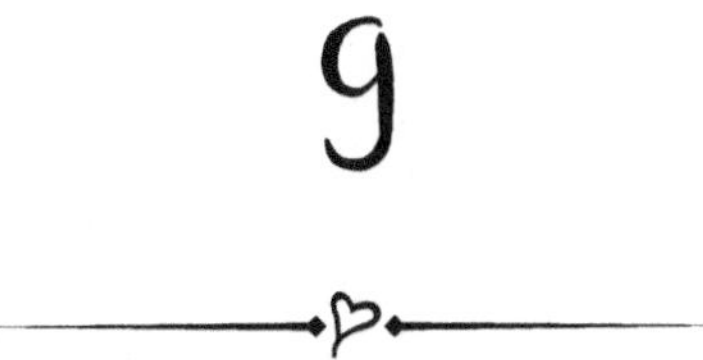

9

The next few days went smoothly, and I continued sitting in the first row. Then one day, the Math professor announced, "Internal exams will begin next Monday."

We were shocked because it felt like college had just started, and now we had only four days left before the exams. None of us had textbooks or reference books for any of the subjects. In a panic, everyone rushed to the library to borrow books using their library cards.

Me, Jeevan, and Amar, who had recently joined Sandy's room, decided to divide and share different subject books to prepare for the upcoming internal exams.

Later in the evening, as I was walking in the corridor, revising for the internals, I noticed Karthik climbing up the stairs.

Karthik noticed me and asked, "Hey, what are you doing? Preparing for the internals?"

I replied, "Yes."

He seemed surprised and questioned, "Why?"

I looked puzzled and asked, "Why what?"

Karthik pulled me inside a room and inquired about the whereabouts of Jeevan and Amar.

"I don't know," I responded.

Karthik insisted that we wait for them to arrive so he could explain something. He told me not to worry about revising and that I would pass the exams.

I was confused about what Karthik was trying to convey and nodded my head, hoping he had some magical way to pass the exam without studying. Perhaps he was referring to cheating? I was getting anxious about it.

"What are you talking about? Tell me," I asked.

"It's a secret. Don't tell anyone, "He said cryptically.

I wondered what this top-secret information could be. Later in the evening, Karthik brought Amar to our room and told us not to take the internal exams too seriously and advised us not to study.

"Why?" Jeevan asked.

Karthik revealed that we could obtain our internal exam booklets after the exam and complete them in our rooms.

This was intriguing and new information for all of us. We learned that many students in our class were doing the same thing.

We became curious and asked, "Who will give us the booklet?"

Karthik explained that each department's peon would provide the booklet in exchange for some money.

"How much does it cost?" we inquired.

Karthik replied, "Each internal booklet costs only 10 rupees."

We were relieved to hear it was affordable and wondered if this plan was foolproof.

We discussed the plan further:

"Did all the seniors do the same thing?" we asked.

"Yes. Everyone in the class knows about this, including girls," Karthik replied.

"Oh, really?" we said in surprise.

"Did Sandy know about this?" I asked.

"No, I didn't tell him. He won't agree with this. Please be careful and don't tell him. We don't know what he might do; he might report it to the principal," Jeevan whispered.

We nodded in agreement.

The day of the math's internal exam arrived, and our professor was already in the lecture hall. I quietly took my favorite seat in the front row, near the middle, facing the professor.

The professor instructed us to place all our bags and notes in front near black blackboard and warned that anyone caught copying would be thrown out of the exam hall.

As the professor wrote questions on the blackboard, I began to read. I realized I didn't know the answers to any of the questions, but I wasn't worried because we would get the booklet after the exam anyway.

I looked back Sandy was writing seemingly focused. I observed Karthik, Jeevan, and Amar, all writing with their heads down.

Doubts began to creep in. Did they deceive me? I checked the questions again and again, unable to remember anything related to the subject. I felt foolish for believing their plan. My hands shook, and my mind went blank.

After the exam, I went to Karthik and asked, "How did it go? Was it good? Did you solve all the problems?"

Karthik replied, "No, I wrote all the questions in the booklet."

Later that day, around 4:30 PM, Karthik came to our room and suggested that we go and collect our papers. We all agreed and paid 10 rupees each to get our booklets. Back in our room, we rewrote all the papers and replaced them.

We followed the same process for all the internal exams, just like everyone else in our class, except for Sandy.

Finally, one day, our internal exam papers were returned. Everyone had done exceptionally well in the exams, except Sandy, who had scored only 16 marks in mathematics. The math professor was a bit surprised, as he had expected Sandy to be the topper this time.

The professor asked Sandy what had happened, expressing his disappointment. Sandy replied confidently, "I'm still the topper, sir. You missed giving 8 marks to this problem," pointing to his booklet.

The professor, puzzled, responded, "But your answer is wrong. It's a solved question in the textbook."

Sandy went to the board and explained, "Sir, the textbook answer is incorrect. If we solve it using a different theorem, the answer is more accurate." He illustrated his point with examples and mentioned a mathematician who had suggested this more precise method.

The professor was astonished, and the entire class fell silent. After a moment, the professor admitted, "I failed to understand this, Sandy. I'll add the 8 marks you deserve." Sandy's score was revised to 24 marks.

professor asked, "Where is the other mark?"

Sandy chuckled and said, "My mistake in a one-mark question."

We were all impressed by Sandy's honesty and ability. In the other subjects, everyone scored well by replacing their papers, but only Sandy had achieved a high score through his own knowledge.

We felt somewhat embarrassed, not because we had cheated in the exams, but because Sandy had shown us the value of honesty. We took an oath not to engage in this type of cheating again.

10

Time flew by, and before we knew it, our first-semester exams were over. As we began packing our bags, Sandy entered our room and asked, "Could we plan a trip?"

We all stared at him, surprised.

"Perhaps a short two-day trip?" Sandy suggested once more.

None of us responded.

We were all taken aback because we had been eagerly anticipating this break to return home.

"You're not going home?" Karthik inquired of Sandy.

"No, I'm coming to your home," Sandy replied.

Karthik casually invited Sandy, saying, "Well, at least I'll have some company there." Little did he know that Sandy would actually accept the invitation to visit his home.

"Alright, first we'll go to Karthik's house. There are some good tourist spots we can visit. After that, we'll head to our homes," Sandy proposed, pointing at us.

Jeevan, Amar, and I remained silent, not quite enthusiastic about the idea.

I shook my head as a sign of disagreement.

Sandy turned to Jeevan and Amar, asking for their thoughts.

They also shook their heads, indicating they weren't interested.

"Okay, Karthik and I will go to his home," Sandy said.

Karthik glanced at us, looking a bit puzzled. He was probably wondering why Sandy wanted to come along.

We couldn't help but stifle our laughter at the situation.

Karthik said reluctantly, "Hey, there are some nice places near my hometown, like the seaside. You guys can visit those and come back."

In the end, Sandy managed to convince us by assuring that it would only be a two-day trip. We reluctantly agreed to visit Karthik's home.

My parents had been eagerly awaiting my return, and after some initial reluctance, I managed to convince them to let me go on the trip. Jeevan and Amar also got the green light from their parents, but Sandy, on the other hand, seemed to have no home to return to. We weren't even sure where Sandy's house was located.

After a long bus journey, we arrived in Karthik's hometown, Siddapura. We were warmly welcomed into Karthik's home. His father was a businessman and a political leader, and they lived in a large and impressive house. It felt like stepping into a palace. Karthik's mom had prepared rooms for us, and we were treated with great hospitality.

Upon our arrival at Karthik's house, it began to rain heavily outside. The downpour was so intense that we were forced to stay indoors. We couldn't venture outside in such weather.

Due to the continuous heavy rain, we spent the day indoors. Fortunately, Karthik's family took good care of us. We enjoyed a delicious dinner and had a comfortable night's sleep. The following morning, the rain showed no signs of letting up, so we had to extend our stay and remain indoors.

While we were gathered at the dining table, Sandy proposed a plan to visit the beach early the next morning if the rain stopped. Everyone agreed. Just then, an unexpected voice chimed in from the kitchen, saying, "I also want to join you."

We all turned our heads, Karthik's mother Chetana Aunty was standing there. Karthik, looking a bit flustered, muttered, "Mom."

His mother, with a hopeful expression, asked if she could join us.

Karthik, appearing frustrated, replied, "Mom, we friends are going. What would you do at the beach?"

"Let Aunty also join us, what is the problem" Sandy intervened

"Please don't tell to your father that I am also joining" Mom murmured.

Karthik gave her a harsh glance.

We all were ready to go to the beach, which was 60 km from Karthik's town. After an hour-long journey, we arrived at the beach.

It was the most beautiful beach I had ever seen, with the waves crashing gently on the shore. We all began to walk along the beach, taking in the serene atmosphere.

"I never imagined I would be standing on this beach," Chetana Aunty remarked.

Sandy added, "I hope it won't rain."

"It is already raining in my mind," Chetana Aunty laughed heartily.

Sandy then suggested, "There is a water motorbike. Is anyone interested in trying it?"

Before anyone could reply, Karthik's mom shouted from behind, "I am!"

It looked quite scary, and we all turned our attention to Karthik, who was clearly embarrassed and unsure of how to react. Before Karthik could say anything, his mom headed towards the sea.

Sandy also began moving towards the water.

"Are you mad, Mom?" Karthik yelled in concern.

However, she ignored his pleas and was thrilled, unable to contain her excitement to enter the water. I held Karthik from behind and asked him to wait.

Sandy hopped onto the water motorbike, with Karthik's mom sitting behind him. Sandy started the bike, and it began speeding up. After a while, we could see that they had gone quite far from the shore.

Karthik became extremely anxious and held onto my hand tightly. He didn't want his mother to go with Sandy, and he was worried about her safety.

They went so far that they became barely visible. Even the fishermen and other people in boats appeared nervous, judging by their expressions. Amar and Jeevan were looking around, trying to figure out where they had gone, while Karthik was pacing back and forth, searching for them.

After some time, we spotted Sandy returning to the shore. However, we soon realized that Karthik's mother had fallen into the sea, and Sandy seemed to be ignoring her, heading back to shore.

We all became anxious and rushed towards Sandy as he approached the shore.

11

"Where is Chetana Auntie?" I yelled at Sandy.

Sandy just laughed and turned to look back at the sea.

Karthik couldn't contain his frustration and pushed Sandy from behind. "Are you mad?" he asked angrily.

Sandy, acting as if nothing had happened, calmly inquired, "Wait, what happened?"

I was irritated and noticed a push pole lying nearby. Without thinking, I grabbed it and hit Sandy on the head with it.

Sandy, holding his head in pain, fell onto the seashore. Jeevan, Amar, and Karthik were shocked and yelled at me, asking why I had hit him.

I panicked and shouted back, "He's the problem for everything!"

They turned their attention to Sandy, who was unconscious. Amar quickly grabbed some water and poured it on Sandy's face and head, but he didn't wake up. Fear surged through me, and I clung to Sandy, crying and regretting my actions.

Suddenly, we heard a voice from behind. I turned around and saw a lady with wet clothes and hair approaching us.

"Are you okay, Mom?" Karthik rushed to hug his mother.

Realizing that nothing had happened to her, I cursed myself for hitting Sandy.

"What happened to Sandy? Why is he lying there?" Chetana Aunty asked.

"We need to take him to the hospital immediately!" I exclaimed.

We hurriedly lifted Sandy and placed him in a vehicle, rushing to the nearest hospital. I kept blaming myself for what I had done.

At the hospital, Sandy lay unconscious on the bed while the doctor administered injections. We anxiously waited for hours, filled with worry and regret.

We all waited for hours, praying to God that Sandy would be okay. I couldn't shake off the guilt that if something happened to Sandy, it would be my fault.

Karthik asked his mother, "How did you fall into the sea?"

His mother replied, "No, I didn't fall; I jumped voluntarily."

"Are you mad, Mom? Because of you, all this happened today," Karthik scolded her.

I didn't know how to react, and I remained silent.

After a while, Sandy regained consciousness. I went up to him and said, "Sorry, Sandy."

"You hit me pretty hard, man!" he remarked.

"Sorry," I apologized again.

“Karthik's mother returned, She is fine”, I informed him about Aunt's return.

"I knew that; she was bound to come back," Sandy remarked.

I asked, "How?"

Sandy laughed and said, "Yes, she belongs to an aquatic family."

Amar, Jeevan and I exchanged puzzled glances. I muttered, "Another nonsense."

Karthik and his mother entered the room, and she asked Sandy if he was okay.

"I'm fine, Mom. One more round?" Sandy jokingly suggested.

Karthik lowered his head and said, "Sorry, Sandy."

Sandy pointed at me and playfully threatened, "Why are you saying sorry? This guy is the one who hit me with the pole. I'll take my revenge on him!"

Jeevan interjected, "We were worried that something had happened to Auntie."

"It's better if we head back our home now and we will check with the doctor about your discharge" Amar suggested.

Sandy asked, "Why? What's the urgency? We can stay here in the hotel tonight. You guys are asking a marine creature to live on land. That's not fair."

"No more jokes, please. We've been through enough. Let's go back," Karthik exclaimed.

12

As I sat in the vehicle, I couldn't help but reflect on how insightful Sandy was. He seemed to understand people at a deeper level, something we often missed. He had recognized Karthik's mom's true nature, while even her own son, Karthik, hadn't fully understood her.

Sandy's talk of different "family fundas" and his belief that Karthik's mom was a marine creature were bizarre, but I found myself contemplating their validity. After all, Karthik's mom had displayed such genuine happiness at the sea, and Sandy seemed so sure.

I called Jeevan and Amar into the vehicle and shared my thoughts. "I think we should stay back here. Maybe Sandy is right," I told them.

Jeevan's face turned red, and he protested, "What are you saying? You want us to let Auntie swim in the sea? Do you know how dangerous that is? He's insane!"

"But he's saying she's a marine creature, and she looked so happy coming back from the sea. There's something different about it," I argued.

"What if something goes wrong? Who'll be responsible then?" Jeevan retorted.

"Can you go and convince Karthik?" I asked Jeevan.

"We need his agreement."

Jeevan and Amar approached Karthik, who was sitting next to Sandy's bed while his mother gazed at the sea from the window.

"Have you convinced Karthik?" I asked Jeevan when they returned.

"Who needs his agreement, Sandy already decided to stay back" Jeevan replied.

"When Mom is swimming, we'll follow her in an escort boat with swimming experts," Sandy informed us.

We went to the seashore and arranged for boats and swimming experts. The weather for the next day was also looking fine.

Now, the most challenging part of Sandy's plan lay ahead: convincing Auntie to wear a swimsuit. She was initially reluctant, worried about how she would look at her age.

"Why worry? It is full length swim suit. You can't swim in a saree for long distances. Besides, I'm planning a big event for you, Mom. Try to understand," Sandy reassured her.

"But wearing a swimsuit at my age... it doesn't feel right," Auntie expressed her concerns.

Sandy tried to ease her worries, saying, "Don't worry.

You might feel shy for just the first 5 minutes. After that, I guarantee you'll be comfortable."

Karthik decided to distance himself from this endeavor. Sandy eventually managed to convince Auntie to wear the swimsuit.

13

In the morning, around 6 o'clock, we had initially planned to start, but the cold weather outside delayed us until around 7 o'clock when we finally headed to the beach.

Auntie was wearing a full length swimsuit with a gown over it.

We were unsure which direction to take, so we asked Auntie for guidance. Sandy suggested heading straight ahead.

Karthik voiced his concerns, asking, "Mom, do you think all this is necessary?"

Auntie shared her dream from her youth, explaining, "I had a dream of crossing this sea when I was young. We won't go too far, just around 2 km, and then we'll return."

We all boarded one boat, but Karthik chose not to join us. Each boat had a swimming expert onboard.

As we were preparing to enter the water, Sandy was giving Aunty a final briefing. We noticed a vehicle approaching us, and I nervously kept my eyes on it. Suddenly, Karthik's father stepped out of the vehicle, causing me to take a deep, anxious breath.

He walked toward Aunty, who turned and saw him. She became frightened and started moving backward. Suddenly, Karthik's father grabbed her hair and began to drag her forcefully. She fell onto the sand, but he didn't stop. It was an awkward and disturbing sight, and Sandy remained silent, simply observing.

Karthik rushed to his mother's side and pleaded with his father to let go. His father finally released her. Karthik then helped his mother to the vehicle, and his father drove away.

Karthik stood some distance away, and then he walked toward the vehicle we had brought.

Sandy settled the payment for the guards we had arranged and sent them back. Meanwhile, Amar, Jeevan, and I waited for Sandy, unsure of what to do. Sandy went to smoke.

"He always seems to bring trouble," I muttered to Jeevan and Amar.

"How did Karthik's father come to all these things?" Jeevan asked.

I pondered for a moment, wondering how he found out.

"I think Karthik must have called and told him," Amar replied.

"But why would he do that?" I wondered.

"He was probably worried, It's a very dangerous thing to do. If something happened to Karthik's mother, we could all end up in jail. This might be better than the alternative." Amar replied.

"But why doesn't Sandy understand the risks he's putting us and Aunty through?" I questioned.

"He did mention something about her being from an aquatic family," Jeevan chuckled.

"What should we do now?" I asked.

"We'll go back to Karthik's home, collect our bags, and then head to our hometown," Amar proposed.

"What about Sandy?" I inquired.

"He'll stay back in the hostel," Jeevan replied.

"It's strange, isn't it? He doesn't have a home; he's an orphan. Is it? Amar asked

"What If he wants to come with us?" I wondered.

"I won't take him with me," Jeevan declared. "He might create another scene there."

"We won't tell him. We'll just escape from the hostel," Amar suggested.

"Can we face him when we return from vacation?" I asked

.

"I don't know what we'll do then," Jeevan admitted.

We made our way toward the vehicle. Karthik was already inside, waiting for us. We climbed in and sat in silence, avoiding eye contact with Karthik, who had his head down.

I broke the silence, asking Karthik, "Who called your father here?"

Karthik remained silent.

"You did the right thing, Karthik. If something had happened to your mom, we all would've been held responsible," Jeevan reassured him.

Karthik still didn't respond.

We noticed Sandy approaching the vehicle and silently watched as he got in.

With everyone onboard, Karthik started the vehicle, and we began moving. None of us spoke during the ride.

Karthik stopped at the lodge where we had stayed the previous night.

We gathered our luggage and checked out of the hotel. It was already 10 o'clock in the morning, and Sandy was standing below, smoking.

As we were about to get into the vehicle, Sandy told us, "You guys go have breakfast and come back. I'll wait here."

"You're not having breakfast?" I asked.

"No, I won't eat until Aunt's swimming dream is fulfilled," Sandy declared.

We were all taken aback and frightened. We exchanged anxious glances. Sandy seemed unwilling to let go of this matter, and to me, he started to resemble a troublemaker.

In a fit of frustration, Karthik slammed his hand hard on the vehicle and shouted in agony, "Can someone please tell me what's going on?"

"Why are you so angry?" Sandy inquired.

"You! Why do you want to endanger my mother's life?" Karthik yelled.

"She is not only your mother; she is my mother also!" Sandy shouted back.

We were all shocked, seeing Sandy this angry for the first time. Fear gnawed at us.

Karthik began to weep, and I went over to comfort him.

"Can't we just drop this matter?" Jeevan shouted at Sandy.

"No, I will not," Sandy firmly replied.

"What do you want, Sandy?" Jeevan shouted once more.

"I will not stay quiet until I fulfill my mother's dream," Sandy replied firmly.

We all fell into a tense silence.

I put my hand on Karthik's shoulder and guided him inside the hotel, with Jeevan and Amar following us. We sat down on a bench, feeling lost.

"What should we do now?" Karthik asked, his voice full of uncertainty.

We were all aware that Sandy wouldn't let this matter go. Whatever he had in mind, he was determined to see it through. The question was how to escape this situation.

"I made a mistake by informing my father... I did it out of fear that something would happen to my mother," Karthik admitted.

"Wait... maybe Sandy has a plan. He knows how to handle situations like this. Don't worry, I think he'll find a way to convince your father," I reassured him.

Karthik wasn't convinced. "No, it's not possible. You don't know my father. He's a very strong-willed person. I didn't tell him about this. It's all happening because of Sandy, and Sandy has brainwashed my mother. Our family has a good reputation, and my father won't tolerate any of this. If he finds out it's because of Sandy, he won't spare him."

I sighed. "On one side, your father is strong, and on the other side, Sandy is equally strong. What can we do now?"

Amar suddenly suggested something shocking. " we have to kill Sandy The only solution we have is to get rid of Sandy."

We all reacted with shock. "What are you saying?" we yelled at him.

Amar stuck to his point. "There's no other option."

"I have a plan," Karthik declared.

"What plan?" I asked, curious about what he was thinking.

Karthik's response, however, shocked us all. He said, "We will push Sandy from the moving vehicle...!!"

Jeevan couldn't contain his shock and anger, shouting, "Are you people mad... He is our friend!"

Karthik responded sharply, "She is my mother."

"But he is not planning to kill her," Jeevan argued.

Karthik remained resolute, saying, "But he is taking her to swim in this ocean... do you think she will come back after going into the deep sea?"

"But he is not taking your mother... your mother only wanted to swim... what he did, he just supported her," Jeevan emphasized.

Karthik, however, was still concerned about how his father would react, and he expressed it by saying, "I know... my mother is mad... my father is a reputed man. At this age, his wife wearing a swimming suit will embarrass him."

Jeevan continued to stress that violence was not the answer, saying, "But that is not the reason to kill Sandy... How can you think like this about your friend?"

Karthik then turned to Jeevan and asked for an alternative solution, "You suggest any other options?"

Jeevan proposed a less drastic plan, "Instead of going to your home, we can go to the college hostel... Sandy will not come to your house again."

Karthik, still unsure, sought assurance, "Are you sure Sandy will not come back again?"

Everyone waited for Jeevan's response, hoping that it would provide a solution to the escalating conflict.

Jeevan, after giving it some thought, responded, "I am guessing so."

However, Karthik remained resolute, stating, "No, he will not leave this matter until my mother crosses this ocean or my mom should tell him that she is not interested in crossing this."

Jeevan tried to reason with Karthik, saying, "Are you joking? Crossing an ocean is not easy, so he said only 2 km."

Karthik countered, "Ya, I know this time he told me 2 km, but my mother wants to go deep as much as possible. Sandy was talking about setting a record by crossing it. I heard that when they first saw this ocean."

Jeevan seemed unsure about the next steps, and he asked, "Then what do we do now?"

Karthik emphasized, "Somehow we should not allow him to come to my house. If my father comes to know he is supporting my mother, he will kill him."

we decided to head directly to the hostel instead.

After leaving you guys in the hostel, I will come back to my home, and you people should somehow manage to keep Sandy at the hostel.

"We all agreed and went back to the vehicle," but Sandy was not in the vehicle.

We saw him smoking at a nearby shop.

"Sandy Sandy..." I yelled at him...

He came back with a cigarette in his hand. We all sat inside the vehicle, and Karthik started the vehicle.

"Is your planning over?" Sandy asked.

I was stunned and replied, "What plan?"

"Don't forget I am an eagle... Karthik, don't become too smart. Go to your home," he told us.

I was wondering how he knew our plans. We all started feeling anxious again.

" "Don't come to my home. If you act smart there, my father will kill you," Karthik warned Sandy.

Sandy remained unfazed. "I know how to handle your father, don't worry."

Karthik continued to question Sandy, "What do you know about my father? He's very strong and won't hesitate to harm anyone who gets in his way. I'm warning you for your own safety; leave it be. Even if my mother's dream doesn't come true, it won't affect you."

"Your father is Felidae family. I know how to handle them ... you don't worry ... I will take care ..."

"Why do you want to risk my mother's life and bring chaos into our peaceful life?" Karthik yelled at Sandy once more.

"You fool, anyway, your mother is going to die. Your father doesn't give any respect to your mother. Women in such families have no individual respect. What your mother receives from your father is nothing short of ill-treatment. When a woman gets married, she expects her life is going to improve. Your mother had similar hopes from the marriage, but what your father did..."

Sandy, however, had a different perspective. He defended his position, explaining.

He went on, "Your mother excelled in school, and she's had a dream since her school days of swimming in this ocean. But she never received encouragement from her parents. She was married to your father at a young age, and she's been dreaming about this day and night ever since. Her body craves water, and if she wants to swim, it's just a matter of an hour. Why are you all not allowing her?"

"I am worried because if something happens to her..." Karthik said.

"Are you people mad? I'm telling you, she comes from an aquatic family. Nothing will happen to her..."

"Do you know how dangerous swimming in the ocean is? You have to make many preparations before attempting open-water swimming. It's not child's play. You are risking my mother's life for your unrealistic dreams. I will not allow this," Karthik said firmly.

"I know the unpredictability of nature, and I also understand that safety is extremely important. I know physicians and emergency medicine are required. We need lifeguards and watercraft, and I know it's a solo sport. We need to take the opinion of the atmospheric administration on today's climate.

We have arranged for some lifeguards and watercraft; I haven't bothered about other precautions because we need to worry about them when humans are swimming. For marine creatures, this is not necessary," Sandy replied.

"Don't repeat the same nonsense logic," Karthik yelled.

"Yesterday, when we visited your home, I couldn't help but notice some interesting details. In the backyard, there's a sizable swimming pond, and in every room, including the kitchen, there are aquariums. What struck me as unusual was how your mom, while cooking, would reach her hand out of the window when it was raining. Additionally, I observed her placing a tray of water beneath her leg while she cooked in the kitchen. These behaviors piqued my curiosity. She seemed exceptionally joyful when it rained, and her excitement was evident when she enthusiastically jumped from the kitchen to the dining table upon hearing about our beach trip.

When I was taking her on the water motorbike, she couldn't resist the temptation and jumped into the sea. Water was her true sanctuary, her second home". Sandy explained

"I plead with you, please don't come to my home," Karthik implored Sandy.

Sandy remained quiet for a moment, and then replied, "Okay, we'll go back to the hostel. But take care of your mother, and you need to get back home as soon as possible. You can drop us off at the nearest bus stop."

"I can drop you at the hostel," Karthik offered.

"No, it's dangerous for your mother to be alone," Sandy insisted.

"Why... why are you saying that?" Jeevan interjected.

"These families tend to be emotionally fragile, making hasty decisions," Sandy explained. "I suspect your mother might have attempted something like this before."

Karthik's face turned red, and he accelerated the vehicle.

"Stay cool, Karthik. I hope nothing will happen. But make sure you stay with your mom and never leave her alone," Sandy advised.

"Okay," Karthik replied.

Karthik stopped the vehicle at the bus stop ... we all got down there.

Karthik moved with the vehicle

15

It was around 11 o'clock in the morning, and we found ourselves sitting at the bus stop under the bright sun. Sandy kept looking upwards, and it was unclear what had caught his attention. Amar, Jeevan and I decided to go to a nearby tea stall to have a tea, while Sandy stepped aside to smoke a cigarette. Since it was a village, it appeared that only one or two buses passed through each day.

After enjoying our tea, we returned to the bus stop and took a seat. We noticed several private vehicles passing by on the main road.

"I think we should stand on the main road to flag down one of these private vehicles, Let's step outside," I suggested.

We all headed out. However, when we looked around, Sandy was nowhere to be found. Concerned, I turned to Amar and Jeevan, asking, "Do you guys have enough cash to get home? I only have 50 rupees left."

Jeevan and Amar began searching their pockets, and when we pooled our money, we found that we only had a total of 110 rupees.

Amar exclaimed in frustration, "How are we going to get home? Why is Sandy causing so many problems for us?"

"He must have gone to Karthik's home again. What should we do now?" I asked.

Amar suggested, "We should just head home. We only have a few days of vacation left, and all of this trouble is because of him. Now he's disappeared with all our money."

Jeevan added bitterly, "We should have just gone along with the plan to push him out of the vehicle."

"There must be a reason; otherwise, he wouldn't just leave like this," I speculated.

Amar retorted, "What reason could there be? We were all inside; he could have at least informed us before taking off."

"Wait a minute, he was looking at something in the sky repeatedly," I recalled.

We all turned our gaze to the sky, but it appeared bright and ordinary to us, with nothing out of the ordinary in sight.

"What would be the ticket fare from here to the hostel?" Jeevan asked.

Amar shrugged. "Not sure."

"Hey Hey," there was a voice from behind. We turned around to see the pan shop owner calling us, waving his hand and gesturing for us to come over.

We approached the shop owner, and he handed us 500 rupees. We were shocked.

"What is this?" I asked.

"Money," he replied. "Your friend told me to give it to you."

"He asked you to come to Siddapura," he added.

We accepted the money and headed back to the main road.

"Have you ever met such a peculiar guy like Sandy in your life?" I asked Jeevan.

Jeevan shook his head in disbelief.

"What is this nonsense...? I will not go there again. Karthik himself told us not to come to his house. Still, we are going... What are we actually doing and why are we doing this, wasting our vacation and not going to our homes?" I exclaimed.

"You guys want to go to Siddapura?" I asked.

"No," both Amar and Jeevan replied.

"Alright, let's go back to hostel," I suggested.

"I hope this money is enough to get us there."

We stood by the side of the main road, waiting for the next private vehicle. We waited for more than half an hour, and we all became tired.

"We won't lose anything by going to Siddapura," Jeevan muttered while looking at the other side.

I noticed that Jeevan was changing his mind.

"Are you crazy? I'm not coming. You can go. If he wanted us, why did he leave us here and go alone?" Amar argued.

"He doesn't want to waste his time," I explained.

"What do you mean?" Amar asked.

"We wouldn't have agreed if he had told us to go back to Karthik's house. We would have wasted his time arguing. There's something wrong. He wanted to go urgently," Jeevan theorized.

"Stop all this," Amar told to Jeevan.

Initially, Jeevan wanted to go, but Amar and I rejected the idea. Eventually, we gave 200 bucks to Jeevan. After a while, I started thinking about why Sandy had left in a hurry. There must be a reason; otherwise, he wouldn't have acted this way. I tried to convince Amar, and finally, he agreed. All three of us decided to go to Siddapura.

After reaching Siddapura, we went to Karthik's house, and it was around 3 o'clock. We rang the doorbell, and a maid answered the door.

We inquired about Karthik, and she informed us that they were at the hospital. Karthik's mother was unwell.

Shocked, we obtained the hospital's address and hurried there.

Our hearts were heavy, and it felt hard to breathe. I wanted to scold Sandy for leaving us like that, but deep down, I knew he had a reason. We rushed to the hospital and found Karthik and Sandy standing near a room.

They didn't appear surprised by our arrival; they simply gazed at us. Amar asked about Aunt's condition, and Karthik informed us that she is fine now. We didn't want to pry into the details, so we sat silently on a bench for a long time.

Eventually, Karthik suggested that we go home and get some rest. We returned to his house, and we noticed that his father wasn't there, which seemed strange. We asked the maid about his whereabouts, and she mentioned that he had an election campaign to attend that day.

The next day, in the afternoon, Sandy and Karthik brought Aunty back home. She smiled at us, We still didn't know what had transpired, but we noticed that all the large aquariums had been removed from the house, which struck us as odd.

After leaving Auntie in a room, Karthik came out, and Sandy remained inside with her. This gave us a chance to talk to Karthik. I asked him, "What actually happened?"

Karthik replied, " I don't know either. Before I arrived here, Sandy was already here. He's the one who took Mom to the hospital." This revelation left us all stunned, and I couldn't help but think that Mom had attempted suicide. If Sandy hadn't been here, we might have lost her.

"Did your father know about this?" I asked Karthik, seeking clarification.

"No, Sandy didn't allow me to inform him," Karthik explained.

"Why?" I inquired further.

Karthik responded, "He told me it would worsen the situation." Just then, Sandy called Karthik inside the room.

"How did Sandy arrive before you?" Jeevan inquired.

"He took a lift on the bike it seems, which has a shortcut route to reach here," Karthik clarified.

Karthik entered the room, and we followed him in quietly. He asked his mom, "Mom, are you okay?"

His mom began to cry and opened up, "I don't know if I'm okay or not. Please forgive me for troubling you so much. I know your father loves me a lot, but I hate to stay away from the water. I can't explain what happens to me when I see water. I find such joy in it. I don't know if there's anyone else like me out there. It's like an addiction. Sometimes I wonder if it's in my genes."

She continued, "If you love something deeply and can't have it, wouldn't you be depressed? It's the same for me, but very few people can understand what I'm going through."

16

We returned to the hostel with Sandy. Jeevan, Amar, and I decided to extend our stay with Sandy for one more day before heading back home. Sandy was feeling quite upset, blaming himself for Chetana Aunt's situation. He believed that if he hadn't provoked her inner desire to swim, she wouldn't be in this predicament.

After a day had passed, Karthik called us at the hostel warden's phone and informed us that his mother was missing. His father had filed a missing report with the police. We were all stunned and uncertain about how to respond

Sandy felt even more shattered, thinking that he was somehow responsible for all of this. We decided to stay with Sandy for another day, unsure of what to do next.

We continued to stay in the hostel, coming up with various excuses to convince our families. The second semester started and passed quickly, but there was still no news of Karthik's mother, and the police had made no progress in finding her. Almost a year flew by as we completed our third semester. However, during this time, we noticed a significant change in Sandy. His once cheerful demeanor had been replaced by constant worry and concern for Chetana Aunt, whose mysterious disappearance weighed heavily on his mind. During our breaks between the second and third semesters, Sandy took it upon himself to conduct searches in various cities near Siddapura, especially those cities with rivers and seashores. He really wanted to discover any sign of her, but despite all his hard work, there was no trace of her.

One morning, during our fourth semester, as Jeevan and I were making our way from the hostel towards the road, we noticed our senior, Jyothi, calling out to us from the other side of the road. She was standing there with a foreigner. As we approached them, she explained that the foreigner was inquiring about your friend Sandy. We both looked at him in amazement. He stood tall at 6 feet and had fair skin.

"Do you know Sandy?" the foreigner asked.

Jeevan and I exchanged puzzled glances.

"Yes, we do," Jeevan replied.

"You know, you know," he repeated, clearly surprised.

"Where is he?" he inquired once more.

"He's here in the hostel."

"Oh, is that so? I inquired at the college office, and they told me there is no student named Sandy."

"Yes, that's correct. His real name is Sandeep Kumar, but we all call him Sandy," I explained.

"Oh, is it? Can you take me to him?" he pleaded.

We entered the room, and Sandy was fast asleep.

"Sandy, someone wants to meet you," I said.

"He's Sandy," we introduced Sandy to the foreigner.

"Hey, I'm John," the foreigner introduced himself.

We asked him to take a seat.

"Do you know Chetana?" He asked Sandy.

We were all surprised, wondering what had happened to her.

"Yes, we know her. What happened to her?" Sandy asked, his agitation clear.

"Nothing serious. She sent me here," John replied.

"Can you come with me?" he asked Sandy.

"Where?" Sandy asked.

"To my home." He said

"Why?" Sandy asked again.

"Chetana is there," John replied.

"How did you find her? Why is she there?" Sandy inquired.

John went on to explain, "

I'm presently in India for a vacation, and I came here to enjoy my time. I'm part of the Channel Association, and I work as a pilot for open water swimmers. I've helped many swimmers set records while serving as their pilot. One day, as I was out at sea in my boat, taking in the beauty of the ocean, something caught my eye. I witnessed an object falling from the mountain ahead and disappearing into the water. At first, I thought it was just a rock, but then, to my astonishment, a woman emerged from the water with a radiant smile. She was fearlessly swimming in the deep sea. I never imagined someone could survive a fall from such a massive mountain."

"I immediately went after her, pulled her into my boat, and now she's staying with us, along with my wife. I've observed that she's an exceptional swimmer, perhaps one of the best I've ever seen," John added.

We were all in awe of Chetana's swimming prowess.

"One day I asked her, 'How did you end up jumping from such a high mountain?'" John began.

He continued, recounting Chetana's response, "She told me she didn't jump; she was pushed."

"Pushed? Who" we all exclaimed.

He went on, sharing Chetana's words, "Her husband," she had confided, and She believed that if she went back home, he would kill her. So, she chose to live with us instead."

"I asked her why her husband pushed her and tried to kill her," John continued. "She explained that he was running for election, and if her swimming and any associated controversies were to make the news, it could jeopardize his chances of winning. So, he told her to 'go and live with your water' and pushed her. She didn't want to file a complaint against her husband. In fact, she said she would be happy if her swimming could help him win the election. That's when I got an idea, and for that, I need your help."

"I want her to swim the English channel. I am sure she will set a world record; no one can beat her. Her world record will bring so much name and fame that it will only enhance her husband's image, and he will win," John said passionately.

Sandy was concerned, "It all needs a lot of money. But who is going to sponsor her?"

Without hesitation, John responded, "I am ready to sponsor her."

John was fully committed to sponsoring Chetana and making all the necessary arrangements for the English Channel swim.

He added, "The only problem now is the weather. In this season, solo swimming is not attempted. We are returning to our country soon. So, you'll have to bring her after two months. I will make all the arrangements. But we have to achieve this before the election. She believes in only you, Sandy, and that's why she sent me here."

Luckily, on that day, Karthik was not there. We decided to keep this a secret and not tell Karthik about the plan.

Finally, after two months of preparations, Sandy and Chetana Aunty were ready to fly. John had sponsored everything, from visas to passports, and they headed to the United Kingdom for this daring adventure.

17

Sandy and Chetana had arrived a day early to scout the beach, preparing for the upcoming challenge of her solo swim. "You are a born swimmer, with only a few hours left to make you a famous woman in the world," Sandy exclaimed to Chetana as they stood on the Dover side, gazing at the cliffs of Cap Gris-Nez beach.

Chetana sat on a sea rock, as she listened to Sandy's encouraging words. Her eyes were fixed on the mesmerizing rhythm of the waves. The icy-cold water of the deep blue sea gently wash over her bare feet before retreating gracefully back into the vast expanse of the ocean. The clear blue sky above seemed to be amused by the middle-aged lady's daring adventure. The weather was perfect, with the sun casting a warm and inviting glow over the scene.

Each echo of the waves reminded Chetana of the unexpected turn her life had taken. Destiny had led her to this very moment, and now, her past hardships and life's cruelties held no significance. All that mattered was the vast expanse of water before her. The echo of the waves served as an irresistible invitation, urging her to let go of the burdens she had carried for so long. With determination in her heart, Chetana dived into the sea. Her body moved gracefully through the cold water as she swam. With each stroke, she felt herself shedding the weight of her worries and doubts, finding relief in the embrace of the ocean.

As they took in the surroundings, the beach appeared to be a peaceful paradise, with people of all ages enjoying its beauty. Kids played happily in the sand, creating sandcastles and chasing each other with boundless energy. Adults relaxed in their swimsuits, basking in the sun's warmth, wearing happy smiles as they soaked in the calming beach atmosphere.

As the evening descended, Chetana found solace in the soothing melodies of live music echoing through the hotel lobby. The tunes washed over her, washing away the nagging doubts that had plagued her for tomorrow's swim. In this moment, she found respite and a renewed sense of purpose.

The following morning, at the crack of dawn around 3 a.m., they all prepared for the big event. John, a crew member, guided Chetana to get ready. Within just 10 minutes, she transformed from her traditional sari attire into a one-piece swimsuit. Yet, despite this swift change, it felt like this moment took 40 years in the making.

As she put on the swimsuit and came out, Chetana couldn't help but feel exposed, as if she were standing there naked in front of strangers. However, what surprised her was the fact that nobody seemed to care about how she looked in her swimsuit. People were so absorbed in their own lives and activities that they scarcely noticed her. This was a stark contrast to her experiences in India. Back in India, even when women wore traditional dresses for bathing (since swimming for women was uncommon), they would still attract unwanted attention and ogling from onlookers. Chetana couldn't help but imagine how her mother might have reacted if she had seen her wearing a swimsuit. In a moment of doubt, she instinctively touched her cheek, half-expecting a slap that never came.

John applied grease and petroleum jelly all over her body, which made Chetana feel quite uncomfortable with his touch. The rubber cap posed a challenge due to her thick, uncut hair that hadn't been trimmed since birth. Sandy and the crew assisted Chetana in making sure the cap fits perfectly. When she looked at herself in the cap, with her hair fully concealed, she couldn't help but feel like she had just shaved her head. This sight prompted her to burst into laughter. It was the first time she had ventured outside without the Kumkum adorning her forehead, and her own face looked strange to her without it. In a sudden moment of panic, she reached into her handbag, desperately searching for her Kumkum tube.

This was the day she had been waiting for, a dream that had been brewing for forty years had finally reached its pinnacle. She had yearned to spend time in the depths of the sea with marine creatures, and sometimes, it felt like water was her only reason to live, her ultimate source of strength, a desire etched into her heart since birth.

The weather conditions appeared to be perfect, and everyone was eagerly anticipating the rise of the sun. She found herself silently praying for the sun to ascend. Even though she was now so close to her dream, past incidents that had dashed her hopes when she was on the brink still haunted her, leaving scars on her life and a lingering sense of apprehension.

Suddenly, at 5 AM, the weather took a turn for the worse. Hazardous tides and high storm surges swept in, catching everyone by surprise. The crew quickly checked the forecast report, which indicated less favorable conditions for the rest of the day. The furious gale was intensifying. Crew member John called Sandy and delivered the unfortunate news, "We will wait for one more hour, but if this persists, we may have to call off the swim."

It was a heart-wrenching moment. They had been eagerly anticipating this day, and just when everything seemed to be going smoothly, it all crumbled away. Every hope they had of getting closer to realizing their dreams appeared to be slipping away with each passing moment. Chetana felt a growing sense of anxiety, and in her desperation, she started chanting Vayu Devata and reciting the Jai Hanuman Chalisa, seeking divine intervention.

After a while, the tides began to recede, but the weather grew colder and colder due to the unusual mist and chilly breeze. The crew had to postpone the swim for another hour.

At 6:45 a.m., Sandy checked John's decision, asking, "What is your decision?"

John, with wide-open eyes, responded, "Looks unfavorable."

The crew, particularly John, was concerned about the cold weather. However, Chetana remained confident in her ability to handle it. Sandy tried to convince the crew, but they were not easily swayed. Eventually, they agreed to proceed with one condition.

"There is always a risk of hypothermia in this weather, so the participant must regularly communicate with us," John explained. "If there are any signs of discomfort, she should immediately inform us. If there is a lack of response, I will call off the swim."

The crew administered an anti-allergic injection to Chetana and provided her with initial instructions. With a heart pounding with fear and doubt, Chetana jumped into the water. As she gazed at her reflection in the water, she questioned herself, "Am I truly from an aquatic family, as Sandy claims? Will I be able to do this?"

Determined to achieve her lifelong aspiration, Chetana reassured herself, "I came this far to fulfill my dream, and I will do it."

The crew, along with Sandy, was ready on the escort boat. Chetana stood before the sea with her arms outstretched, as if she was ready to take flight. After a moment of silence, she waved her hands to signal her readiness. The horn sounded, and with unwavering determination, Chetana embarked on her dream.

18

Chetana began to swim with easy strokes, and as she moved forward, the white cliffs faded away behind her. She found herself enveloped by the deep blue sea below and the expansive blue sky above. The waves of the sea moved around her with serene grace, resembling saintly beings. Her broad chest led the way with unwavering determination, and her strong head kept her body warm and alive. Her powerful legs kicked through the water with purpose. Fearlessness coursed through her, and her body, well-trained and capable, served her faithfully. For her, this was pure and unadulterated pleasure and joy.

Chetana swam on with a keen sense of purpose, not seeking to conquer the water but yearning only to be near to it. Water had always been her most cherished companion, and in its embrace, she forgot all the unbearable struggles and suffering that life had thrown her way.

She swam like a fish. Her legs are outstretched like a frog as she moves. She never knew why she had six fingers in her hand and leg. She now understood how her wider palm and toes are helping her. The body with the fat is keeping her warmth. She felt everything has a reason.

"You used to make a lot of movement in my womb. It was like swimming in my stomach. I used to scream in pain it was very uncomfortable. I suffered a lot because of you" She remembered this is how her mother used to scream at her every time she saw her wet body. She felt this may be indicative of my personality as Sandy says "born swimmer".

Suddenly a big fish scurried her way and Chetana came back from her thought and started blinking in the real ocean world. Ocean swimming was her dream. Her village lake is not so depth. She wanted to sink deeper. She sank and went to the bottom of the sea, what a pleasure it was.....!!. The underwater world was quiet, the fishes were flitted in and out of her body. It was like a movement is a constant thing happening underwater.

John sensing the signals of climate change in the ocean. Air temperature and Water temperature started reducing unseasonably cold.

Half an hour into her swim, Chetana stopped for a food break. She replenished her energy with a warm cup of hot chocolate and a carbohydrate drink. While passing her the water bottle, Sandy asked her, "How are you feeling?" Chetana responded with a serene smile, despite the intense cold.

The chill in the air was unbearable, and her hands trembled as she held the bottle. John, one of the crew members, grew concerned. "I need to know exactly how you are feeling in the water," John inquired.

Chetana pretended to acknowledge his question with a nod, but the distress caused by the cold was clearly evident on her face. John, aware of the worsening weather conditions, began to realize that the swim might be a failure, but he was torn about what to do next.

"I think it is better to call off the swim," John suggested to Sandy.

"We will wait for one more break; if she is not comfortable, we will call it off," Sandy replied.

Sandy encouraged Chetana, saying, "Fill your mind with something else; don't think of the cold. This is a mind game."

"This is your dream," he reminded her.

Chetana took up the challenge, her mind focused on something other than the cold water. She worked hard to recall hazy memories as her hands sliced through the chilly sea. Amid the cold splashes, her mind clung to a single word: "unfortunate daughter." Tears welled up at the corners of her eyes, blending with the saltwater. Her strokes became more fervent and agitated.

Sandy and John watched her with tension, rarely sitting down on the escort boat. They remained vigilant throughout her swim, cheering and using hand signals. At times, Sandy would write succinct messages on a whiteboard, showing it to Chetana. One message simply read "MERMAID."

Chetana couldn't remember when she had learned to swim, but all her childhood memories were intertwined with water. Her eyes brimmed with the recollection of her early years.

ᑭᑭᑭ

Chetana was born into a middle-class family, and her birth was met with disappointment by her mother. Before Chetana's birth, her elder brother had passed away due to an illness. This loss had deeply affected her father, and he had hoped for a boy when her mother became pregnant. However, to their surprise, Chetana was born a girl.

Chetana was born into a family that didn't want a girl. Her father was especially unhappy because he had hoped for a boy. As she grew up, her father treated her badly, often hitting her for no reason and not allowing her to play. Instead of having fun, she had to work hard on the farm, doing tasks that were too difficult for her. This made her arms hurt a lot. While she worked, she would think about her friends having fun at the lake. Chetana never felt her father's love and always felt scared around him.

"How am I responsible for my birth?" Tears welled up in her eyes. Her anger grew, and her swimming strokes became more intense.

Chetana's early experiences with water were marked by her fearless nature. Even as a baby of around 2 years old, she displayed a lack of fear around water while accompanying her mother to the lake, although her mother kept a close eye on her. There were moments when, if left unattended, she would boldly venture into the deeper parts of the lake.

Around the age of 5, Chetana's excitement knew no bounds when she visited a river with her mother. It was like a vibrant playground to her, and her mother couldn't believe her eyes as she watched Chetana brimming with joy. It was tough for her mother to control Chetana as she ran around, jumped into the water, and caused a fuss among the people nearby. Things quickly became chaotic, and two men had to jump in and save her as she tried to go into deeper water. They brought her back and gave her to her shocked mother, who scolded her, "Who told you to jump into the water? Are you crazy?"

Back then, as a child, she didn't fully understand why she had impulsively jumped into the water. She didn't take these incidents seriously at the time. However, in hindsight, she realized that these childhood incidents had left lasting imprints on her subconscious mind.

At the age of around 7, Chetana's mother and she were both expelled from their home, leaving them with virtually no relatives except for a distant cousin brother who lived in a nearby village. Forced by circumstances, they sought refuge in Chetana's uncle's house.

Her aunt treated them like servant maids, never trusting them and refusing to listen to them. She was often ruthless and occasionally violent, especially when her mother made small mistakes. Chetana witnessed her mother's daily tears and had never seen her wear a happy expression. Her mother often went to bed hungry so that Chetana could have something to eat. No matter how hard they worked, her aunt always found reasons to get angry and find fault with them.

Her aunt never allowed them to go outside, constantly yelling and screaming at them. Chetana's mother reached a point where she wished for death, but because of Chetana, she continued to endure each day, despite life growing increasingly miserable as Chetana grew older.

One night, Chetana's mother made the difficult decision to leave their oppressive home. They left for a nearby city and started living on the streets, relying on begging for their survival. They spent weeks in these terrible circumstances.

One day, as they sat hungry on the streets, a cow defecated nearby. Several street boys rushed to collect the dung, which struck Chetana and her mother as strange. Curious, her mother asked one of the boys why they were collecting dung. The boy explained that they sold dung cakes to fill their stomachs.

In time, they were able to construct a simple shelter using old cloth and plastic sheets in an empty space. Their transition to the city marked a newfound sense of freedom after enduring significant hardship in her father's and aunt's house.

In the new city, they started making a living by selling cow dung cakes, and Chetana's mother also enrolled Chetana in a government school.

Chetana vividly remembered her first swim in open water when she was 9 years old. One day, a group of people stormed into the school, demanding that it be closed immediately due to riots heading towards the area. The police were about to impose a curfew, and it appeared that a prominent political leader had been killed in the middle of the road.

Chetana's temporary hut was located a bit far from the school, and all the students were stuck in the school. Curiosity got the better of them as they wanted to know what curfews and riots meant. Chetana and some of her classmates decided to visit Vandana's house, which was very close to the school. However, their teacher did not permit them to go out, as it was not safe for girls at that moment. They all stayed at the school as instructed by the teacher until evening.

As the evening approached and the situation calmed down, the teacher accompanied a few students whose homes were in the same direction and sent them off in groups. Chetana and Shiva, whose houses were in the same direction, left together. After dropping Shiva at his home ,

Chetana had to cross small bridge built over the city lake to reach her hut

While on the bridge, Chetana noticed a group of drunken people approaching from the other side, making a lot of noise. Fear began to consume her, and she wondered what could be happening. As they drew nearer, her heart pounded rapidly, and her fear intensified. No one else was around, and she grew increasingly terrified. In that moment of panic, she remembered her mother's words, "You gave me a lot of pain by swimming in my womb." Overwhelmed by fear, she jumped into the lake, attempting to swim to safety. However, her legs and arms wouldn't cooperate, and she began to sink, screaming for help. Instead of assisting her, the drunken men started laughing, and one of them even threw a stone at her. Horrified, Chetana continued to struggle underwater, moving up and down. Strangely, even after reaching the lakebed, she did not lose consciousness. She fought and started swimming toward the opposite bank of the lake, which was vast and took nearly an hour to reach. No one was in sight as she reached the other side and found herself all alone. The roads were empty, and she didn't know where they led. Exhausted, she slept in the dense grass on the lake's banks.

When she awoke, it was dark, and fear once again gripped the little girl. She knew only one road that led to her home—the road that went over the bridge. So, she jumped into the water again and swam back to the bridge, which took over an hour. Climbing onto the bridge, she took the familiar road back to her home. When she arrived and knocked on the door, Chetana's mother was shocked to see her daughter soaking wet, dressed in wet clothes. Without a word, her mother slapped her across the face, and Chetana couldn't hold back her tears. She hugged her mother tightly.

"Where were you...?" her mother dragged her inside. Chetana felt like she should have stayed in the water itself. No one seemed interested in hearing what had actually happened.

"I knew, one day you would do this, jump in the water. You gave me so much pain in the womb itself," her mother started yelling at her again.

Chetana couldn't bear it. "What have I done wrong?" Her heart started pounding even harder than when she had seen the drunken people on the bridge.

Every time she used to travel on that bridge over the lake, she would secretly wish that the drunken gang would appear again, giving her a reason to jump into the lake. She hoped that the man who had thrown the stone at her would return and throw another stone. If he hadn't frightened her by throwing that stone, she wouldn't have discovered her swimming ability. Everything, she realized, had a reason.

Sandy was another reason she had reached this point. He always used to say, "She is from a marine creature, that's why she's so attracted to the water." And she felt it was true. She had never known why she loved water, fish, and other aquatic creatures so much.

Chetana's voice seemed frozen, her tears mingling with the seawater as she wondered about the state of that small 9-year-old child when she had jumped into the water, how terrified she must have been. What had she done wrong to deserve punishment from her own mother? With all these questions swirling in her mind, she began to sink.

"Are you okay? Are you okay?" The crew started screaming at Chetana as her stroke rate began to slow.

The crew was anxious and asked Sandy to check on her. Sandy yelled, "Mom, Mom, are you okay? Please respond!" They moved the boat closer to Chetana.

After hearing the sound of "Mom, Mom," she snapped back to consciousness and replied, "I am okay."

All the tension among the crew was relieved.

The crew provided Chetana with a carbohydrate drink and a banana while she continued swimming. As she swam and consumed her nourishment, the crew members marveled at the distance she had covered. One of them said to Sandy, "I've never seen such a fabulous swimmer in my entire life."

Sandy replied, "That's the difference between a born talent and a learned skill."

ᑭᑭᑭ

Chetana gradually woke up, transitioning from a dream where she was happily splashing water on her mother. In the dream, her mother shook her head and yelled, "Stop," but with a smile on her face. Chetana laughed and used her hands to wipe her mother's face in the dream. However, as she slowly opened her eyes, she was met with the sight of an angry face holding a broomstick in one hand and yelling, "Wake up." It was a harsh reminder that she was far away from the warmth of her dream, back in the harsh reality of her life.

Chetana stared at her mother with frustration, muttering, "What's wrong with you, Mom?" as she turned to the other side of her makeshift bed. She hoped her mother would leave her alone.

But her mother persisted, urging, "Get away, get the cow dung."

With a tired yawn, Chetana reluctantly got up, knowing that her responsibilities for the day had already begun.

Every day, Chetana collected cow dung from the streets. She followed the wandering cows, often getting into disputes with others over fresh dung as the cows defecated on the streets. Her mother mixed the dung with water and pressed it flat by hand, then sun-dried it to make cow dung cakes. They used these cakes as fuel and also sold them to people in need.

Today, Chetana woke up later than usual, the sun already shining brightly. She rushed to her metal bowl.

"Chai," her mom offered, but with a stern warning, "No swimming today."

Ignoring her mother's words, Chetana hurried outside and spotted Shiva waiting at the corner.

"Sorry I didn't come sooner," Chetana apologized to Shiva.

"We had to go to our swimming lesson," Shiva replied, transferring half of the cow dung from his bowl to Chetana's metal bowl.

Shiva was a year older than Chetana and accompanied her daily to collect cow dung. If she was late, he would collect extra and share it with her to prevent her from getting beaten by her mother.

Chetana was Shiva's teacher when it came to swimming. For the past two months, she had been teaching him, though he still struggled. But he was diligent, always showing up for their lessons. If no one was around at the lake early in the morning, they would swim there; otherwise, they would go to Shiva's field, which had a well with steps leading down to the water and wasn't very deep.

Chetana had a deep love for swimming in the lake, but her mother turned into a monster whenever she found out that Chetana had been near the lake. Throughout her childhood, Chetana's mother kept a watchful eye on her, monitoring her every move. Whenever there was a fair in the city, street dances, gatherings to sing, or the colorful celebration of Holi with men painting their bodies and dancing in the streets, Chetana rarely attended these events. And when she did, her mother always accompanied her. Chetana's mother was extremely protective, never allowing her to swim in public places.

ᑭᑭᑭ

Despite her mother's continuous watch, Chetana continued to visit her friend Shiva's field to swim in the well. After school, she became a regular visitor to that well. As she grew older, her passion for swimming only increased. Chetana's mother was deeply concerned about her marriage.

One day, Chetana and her mother were walking down the road.

"Where are we going, Mom?" Chetana asked.

"Siddapur to see Muthuswamy," her mother replied.

"Why?" Chetana inquired.

"For your marriage," her mother responded.

Chetana protested, "But I have to complete my school, Mom."

Her mother remained silent.

"I'm scared, Mom," Chetana admitted.

"Scared of what?" her mother questioned.

"None of the girls in my class are married," Chetana explained.

"They aren't as restless as you, always jumping into any water you see. Men will be waiting to see you," her mother replied.

As they reached the bus station, a bus was ready to depart for Siddapur.

"Hurry up, get on the bus," her mother urged, pushing Chetana inside.

Chetana was reluctant, her worries growing. She thought that Muthuswamy might be the groom.

"Mom, who is Muthuswamy?" she asked.

"He's a marriage broker," her mother replied.

"Why are you taking me to see him?" Chetana questioned.

"He wants to see you," her mother explained.

After a 30-minute journey, they arrived in Siddapur and went to Muthuswamy's office, where many people were waiting for their turn.

When it was their turn, Muthuswamy greeted them with a friendly smile. They sat down in front of his desk.

He looked at Chetana and asked, "What's your name, baby?"

Chetana felt like saying she wasn't a baby, but she simply replied, "I'm Chetana."

Muthuswamy said, "That's a nice name. Can you tell me what you'd like your future husband to be like?"

She thought, "Oh, I've never really thought about my future husband before. This question feels so strange." And then she started to imagine what kind of husband she'd like to have. She felt that his house should be near the ocean, and she should be able to walk there every day and enter the sea whenever she pleased. He should love her and support her love for the water, unlike her mom. He should have a affection for fish and never eat them, even disliking people who did.

Chetana's dreams for her future husband were centered around her deep connection with the ocean. She didn't consider his height, appearance, or other physical attributes. Her main desire was that he should embrace her passion for water.

Her mother playfully tapped her hand, bringing her back from her daydream. Muthuswamy continued to smile, perhaps intrigued by her unique answer.

"What is your age?" he asked.

"Fourteen," Chetana replied.

He checked her height and took photographs with her and her mother. Muthuswamy mentioned that he would contact them if a suitable match came up.

ᑭᑭᑭ

A few days later, Muthuswamy returned to their hut with a proposal.

"Amma, you are lucky," Muthuswamy exclaimed as he entered the hut.

"Come in, Sir," Chetana's mother welcomed him.

"Say Namaste, you don't know how to greet an elder," she hissed in Chetana's ear while tapping her head.

"Your daughter is going to a good household. You know, a high-class family has taken an interest in her," Muthuswamy said.

"It's all your blessings," Chetana's mother replied.

"They are from your religion," Muthuswamy added.

"Do they know about our situation?" Chetana's mother inquired.

"Yes, I have informed them about your husband and everything. Don't worry; they are not asking for anything except your daughter, Chetana," Muthuswamy reassured her.

"I will always be grateful to them for that," Chetana's mother expressed her gratitude.

"But there's something I want to tell you. Take your time to think about it and give me an answer," Muthuswamy said.

"What is it?" Chetana's mother asked.

"It's nothing serious, just that this groom, Srivastava, is getting married for the second time, and he's only thirty years old," Muthuswamy revealed.

Silence filled Chetana's mother's mind.

"What happened to his first wife?" she inquired.

"She passed away six months ago," Muthuswamy replied.

"You are very fortunate to have such an opportunity. Please take your time and let me know your decision," Muthuswamy said before leaving the hut.

20

Two hours into her swim, Chetana took another break to have some food. She drank hot chocolate and had a carbohydrate drink. Sandy handed her a water bottle and asked, "How are you feeling?" She just smiled and went back into the water, reminiscing about the past.

Every woman dreams that her life will change significantly after getting married. Chetana had similar hopes, but things seemed to have turned sour.

She had married a man who was almost twice her age. On her first day in her husband's house, she was taken to a small, windowless room next to the kitchen. Despite the big house, only three people lived there: Mr. Srivastava, his elderly bedridden mother, and a maid who worked during the day and left in the evening.

Chetana sat in the small room, and suddenly there was a knock on the door. She assumed it was her husband, Srivastava. However, when she opened the door, she saw the maid holding a baby.

The maid smiled and said, "Malkin, take your baby. I am going home."

Chetana was stunned and exclaimed, "My baby?"

"Yes, this is your baby, and you have to take care of it from now on," a voice from the hall replied.

Chetana looked towards the hall and saw her mother-in-law, who was yelling from her bed.

"The first Wife died giving birth to this baby. Saheb married you to take care of this child," the maid whispered quietly.

Chetana felt like the ground beneath her feet had crumbled. She gazed at the baby, who was just six months old, smiling at her.

The maid entered the room with the baby and placed it on the bed. "Muthuswamy never told you about a baby," the maid asked to Chetana.

Chetana shook her head, indicating that she had no prior knowledge of the baby. She was only 15 years old, and this small, windowless room offered her no hope of a new dawn in her life. She turned her face toward the wall to hide her tears and held the baby in her arms, realizing that it was God's decision and there was nothing she could do about it.

Mr. Srivastava never entered her room, never spoke to her, and acted as if she didn't exist. He behaved as if she were a stranger in their home. He had his own room upstairs, and it seemed to Chetana that he had married her solely to have someone to care for his son and his mother.

"Why do you even bother coming home? This isn't a guest house. You just come to sleep and then leave," were the words Chetana's mother-in-law repeatedly hurled at Srivastava whenever he came home. However, he consistently ignored his mother's complaints and headed straight to his room.

Chetana's days were consumed by caring for the baby, her mother-in-law, and managing household chores. Her mother-in-law was very traditional and followed various rituals, including performing pujas before meals. Chetana had to arrange all these rituals for her mother-in-law.

Chetana had become a full-time nurse for both her child and her mother-in-law. As days passed, the exhaustion of looking after them left her with little time to contemplate why her husband never spoke to her or spent time with her.

One day, while her mother-in-law was chatting with their neighbor, Padma Aunty, Padma noticed Chetana and asked, "Is there any good news?"

"No good news," her mother-in-law replied to Padma aunty.

Padma Aunty suggested that Chetana should observe the Solah Somvar Vrat, perform Shiva puja every Monday, and fast on sixteen consecutive Mondays to fulfill her dreams.

The idea of fasting sent shivers down Chetana's spine. She was terrified to revisit a part of life that had been closed off for her. There were days when her mother would say, "It's my fast," as if it were a sacred practice, but Chetana knew that it was because there wasn't enough food for both of them. Sometimes, her mother would fast so that Chetana could have more to eat. Chetana remembered those days when they begged for food, sometimes getting lucky, but often having to make do with just water. After her marriage, she finally had the luxury of eating to her heart's content. She didn't want to experience fasting again because she knew the pain of hunger, the ache of an empty stomach.

Chetana went to the back of the house with Karthik in her lap and sat in the shade. She thought about Padma Aunty's suggestion for the puja. Then, the last words of Padma Aunty came to her mind, "river." She began to recall Padma Aunt's final sentence, "On the 17th Monday, you should visit the river, and all the mud-made lingams should be disposed of in the holy river with a pooja."

Water was the one thing she desired more than anything else in the world. It was a profound moment for her. Chetana returned to the hall and declared, "I will do the pooja, I will fast." Her mother-in-law was delighted.

Chetana commenced the Solah Somvar Vrat puja every Monday according to the rituals. On the 17th Monday, a Brahmin was invited to perform the puja, and several couples and distant relatives were also invited. After completing the puja at home, they all proceeded to the river.

Srivastav's mother insisted that Srivastav accompany Chetana for the puja, and the relatives joined in the insistence. Finally, he agreed.

Chetana, carrying the small child Karthik, Srivastava, her mother-in-law, and all the relatives made their way to the river to perform the puja.

Upon reaching the river, Chetana began to feel a sense of excitement building within her. She had to force herself to stay composed. As she gazed at the water, she felt a deep connection with it, and her mind drifted far away from her present surroundings. She started to imagine herself in the deep water, her thoughts consumed by the river.

The lingams were taken out of a pot and placed on the riverbank for the puja. After the ceremony, the Brahmin instructed Chetana to proceed and immerse the lingams in the holy water. She walked a short distance into the river, with everyone watching her from behind. Then, someone shouted, "Immerse them there!" She bent down and began to lower the lingams into the water to complete the immersion.

Hoping they wouldn't notice, Chetana had intended to immerse herself along with the lingams. While she was plotting her action, a familiar voice came from behind: "Immersed, right? Come back." It was her husband, and it was the first time he had spoken to her.

She stood up, turned, and looked at her husband. He was watching her in silence. Chetana's love for the water was too strong to resist. She readied herself and suddenly fell into the water with her head up, creating a big splash as if a heavy stone had been thrown in. She sank beneath the surface.

Everyone on the riverbank was stunned, thinking she had drowned. They started shouting, "Chetana, Chetana!"

She moved a few feet underwater and then resurfaced. Mr. Srivastava became angry and yelled, "What are you doing? Are you mad?" He felt embarrassed in front of his relatives.

But Chetana paid no attention to all of this. She swam further into the deeper water. Everyone on the bank of the river was in a state of chaos, desperately calling out to her.

Finally, a fisherman on his boat noticed her swimming. He waded into the water and began swimming after her. He reached Chetana and managed to hold onto her, pulling her back to consciousness. Chetana then saw the people standing on the riverbank and remembered why she had come to the river.

With a sense of fear, she made her way back to the riverbank. Mr. Srivastava looked at her with anger, and a concerned relative asked her what had happened. Chetana could only shake her head, as she herself didn't fully understand her actions.

For everyone else, it remained a mystery why she had jumped into the river so suddenly. They believed it to be a miracle, a manifestation of Shiva's grace.

The remaining rituals of the puja, including offerings of coconut, bananas, and betel leaves to all the women present, as well as an aarti performed for the river and for

Chetana, went on as planned. Afterward, they had a meal on the riverbank before heading back home.

Chetana remained silent for the rest of the journey back home. She looked out of the window, tears streaming down her cheeks, as the blue sky seemed to smile at her. This puja hadn't brought her closer to her husband; in fact, it seemed to have made him even angrier with her.

Suddenly, Chetana was hit hard by a high tide, bringing her back to the reality of the ocean world. Despite the initial shock, she found herself enjoying the experience immensely. Her worries were washed away in the cold water, and she felt relaxed, savoring every movement. She flipped, moved up and down, and swam with pure, unbridled enthusiasm, fully immersed in the moment. She was free of all the burdens she had carried with her, feeling entirely herself and truly alive.

After just 5 hours and 52 minutes, Chetana was only a kilometer away from France. Sandy and John were providing encouragement, as this could potentially become a new world record if she managed to conquer this tide.

But then, the tide changed its course, and Chetana was swept backward into the sea. This sudden turn of events filled her with sheer panic.

21

Mr. and Mrs. Srivastav sat in an open car, leading a rally celebrating Mr. Srivastav's election victory with over 60% of the votes. A massive crowd had gathered, waving party flags, cheering, and dancing in exuberance. The air was filled with joyful honking, and it was a scene of jubilation all around.

This was the first time Chetana had joined her husband in such a rally. Although she wore a smile on her face, deep inside, she felt a sense of unease and melancholy. The sudden surge of respect and admiration from society and her husband was hard for her to comprehend. She couldn't help but wonder why winning had changed people's perception of her. She knew that win or lose, she was the same person she had always been. Amidst the cheering crowd, she felt strangely alone.

Her thoughts wandered back to a pivotal moment in her life when Sandy uttered those magical words: "You are a born swimmer." It was the day before a crucial solo swimming event, and Chetana recalled how his words had injected a surge of confidence into her. At that time, her future seemed blurred and uncertain, but Sandy's encouragement had been a guiding light when she felt like she didn't even exist.

She knew how Sandy had played an instrumental role in helping her understand her basic nature and recognize her strength during an unimaginably awkward phase in her life.

As they drove through the city in the rally, Chetana noticed Karthik at the corner of the street, pumping his fists in the air with a proud smile on his face. His eyes were filled with pride and admiration. Chetana waved towards him. The rally took them through various parts of the city, and she felt like she was exploring her own city for the first time. She had rarely been allowed outside before, always confined to the house. It had taken her 40 years to see her own city.

The election had changed Mr. Srivastav's image, largely due to Mrs. Chetana Srivastav's record-breaking achievement in crossing the English Channel faster than any woman before her. This had garnered significant media attention, and it was no secret that her victory had greatly contributed to Mr. Srivastav's election win. He had come to realize this and had taken her along in his campaign as well.

When they returned home, they were surrounded by reporters and cameramen, bombarding them with questions. All the questions were directed at Chetana, causing her to panic.

One journalist asked, "Your husband filed a missing complaint for you. Can you explain why?"

Chetana hesitated but finally replied, "It's been taken back."

"Why was it filed in the first place?" another reporter inquired.

"I wanted to surprise my husband," Chetana replied with a smile.

"Your swimming achievement seemed to help your husband's election campaign. What are your thoughts on that?"

"If it did, I am honored" Chetana responded with a smile.

"Rumors are circulating that your husband attempted to harm you," a reporter stated.

Chetana simply replied, "It's false."

"We've also heard that Mr. Srivastav mentally and physically harassed you," another reporter pressed.

Chetana chose not to comment on that matter.

The reporters then turned to Mr. Srivastav for his comments, but he declined to answer any further questions.

Once they were inside the house, Mr. Srivastav cornered Chetana, holding her by the hair, and looked deeply into her eyes. Chetana saw a connection in his eyes, and he said, "Thank you. You've conquered my world with this achievement. I'm very sorry."

Chetana was shocked, and all her long-buried grief came to the surface as she received a hug from Mr. Srivastav. Tears welled up in her eyes.

After the embrace, Chetana entered her bedroom and collapsed onto the bed. She noticed her red suitcase in the corner and opened it to find her treasures: her black one-piece swimsuit, cap, and waterproof goggles. These were the items she had worn on the day she crossed the English Channel. Holding the swimsuit in her hands, she felt the smooth texture of the fabric. She experienced immense joy and a sense of accomplishment. She realized that this achievement was about impacting how others viewed her, but it shouldn't change who she was. She remembered Sandy's words: "This achievement should not make you think you're invincible. If you do, you're a fool."

She knew that Sandy had wanted to show the world that she deserved better treatment than what she had received. She could see the change in her husband and how he had embraced her. She felt grateful for the transformation in her life. She had once been a helpless woman running away from society and reality, feeling alienated and alone. Now, all of that was behind her, and she was filled with a sense of belonging.

Lost in her thoughts, she was brought back to reality when the swimsuit slipped from her hand and fell to the floor. She gently picked it up, placed it back in the suitcase, and lay back on the bed. She silently thanked Sandy, John, and the English Channel for bringing new life into her existence. Tears welled up in her eyes as she remembered the momentous day when she had conquered the English Channel.

22

Sandy was yelling at Chetana, "Don't worry, you can break this current. Move, move!"

John, on the other hand, was terrified, watching his dream of achieving the fastest swim slipping away with the changing tide. Chetana had been pushed back into the ocean, an hour behind her current point. John tried to cheer her on as he piloted the boat towards her. The distant rocks that had seemed so close earlier were now disappearing from sight. Everything was working against her – the increasing cold, the unusually strong tide, and the grim circumstances.

"You can do it! Use your marine characteristics!" Sandy repeated his encouragement, his voice filled with urgency.

At first, Chetana didn't grasp what Sandy meant by "marine characteristics." In the meantime, another tide came and swept her back another mile, adding to her disappointment. "She'll never break through this tide at this rate," John screamed in sheer terror.

Sandy, growing increasingly nervous, kept shouting at her, "You're a marine creature; you know how to tackle this!"

Suddenly, Chetana spotted a big wave approaching, and just before it could crash over her, she dove down about 50 inches below the surface. To her surprise, the water was much calmer at that depth, and she was able to swim faster. She realized that Sandy was right when he said she was a marine creature. With newfound determination, she pushed herself harder.

John was tense, anxiously searching for Chetana in the water. Sandy reassured him, knowing that Chetana would be safe in the water.

Chetana would surface to breathe and then dive back down when the tide threatened to pull her away. Her stroke rate exceeded 100, and within half an hour, she had covered a distance that had taken her an hour before. She alternated between swimming near the surface and diving below to escape the strong current.

"900 meters!" John finally yelled out to her. Chetana put in a tremendous effort to battle the current, knowing that she was very close to completing her incredible journey. Sandy continued to cheer her on.

With only 300 meters to go, the tide fought hard to carry her away, but Chetana could see the rocks of France in the distance. She finally broke free from the current and reached the rocks.

It was a historic moment, and she had completed the crossing in 7 hours and 4 minutes. Chetana burst into tears, overwhelmed with emotion, while Sandy remained calm. She embraced Sandy, and news of her new world record quickly spread throughout the UK and France.

Chetana received congratulations from numerous swimming legends in both countries, and her achievement made headlines on television, celebrating the Indian woman who had set a new world record by crossing the English Channel

During the live interview, Chetana expressed her gratitude for her husband and son's support, acknowledging their pivotal role in her achievement. She spoke highly of her husband.

Numerous reporters visited Karthik's house, and political leaders greeted Karthik's father. This exposure bolstered his political campaign, increasing his public visibility.

Upon their return, Chetana and Sandy were warmly welcomed at the airport by Karthik and his father. Karthik's father apologized to Chetana, saying, "Forgive me for not understanding you throughout this journey."

Chetana received extensive recognition and support from the government, opening up new opportunities and competitions in swimming. Her lifelong dream of spending time in the water had finally come true, and in every competition, she proved herself to be unparalleled.

The Next Beginning

Our fifth-semester classes had started, and I returned to the hostel on the same day the classes began. I rushed to the hostel to drop off my luggage. It was 8:55 AM, only five minutes left before the class was set to begin. I hurried to the classroom.

As I entered the classroom, I noticed it was already quite full. Sandy and his gang were sitting in the middle of the class. I glanced at my usual first-row seat and noticed a girl sitting there. The girls' row was full, so she had taken the first seat in the boys' row. I thought about going to the back and finding a seat there. However, as soon as I turned to my left to move towards the back, Sandy and Amar started shouting, "First bencher, first bencher!" Karthik and Jeevan joined in, and the entire class turned to look at me, chanting "First bencher." I felt perplexed. I realized that Sandy wouldn't stop until I sat in the first row. So, reluctantly, I returned to the first row and took a seat next to the new girl. She appeared just as puzzled as I was. It seemed like she was new to the college. Once I was seated in the first row, everyone in the class burst into laughter.

We waited for the professor to arrive, and after a while, the girl turned towards me and introduced herself, saying, "Hi, I'm Mukta." My heart started racing, and I felt drained. It was the first time a girl had said hi to me. I managed to smile in response.

She continued, "I transferred here this semester through mutual transfer."

Again, I smiled but couldn't muster the words to respond. Then, the professor walked into the classroom, and the lecture began.

After the class, we returned to our room. I was tired and thought about taking a nap.

Jeevan sarcastically remarked, "Some chit-chat was happening in the first row today."

Amar asked, "Is she new to the college?"

I replied, "Yes, she joined this semester through mutual transfer."

Amar inquired further, "What's her name?"

I answered, "Mukta."

Sandy chimed in humorously, "Looks like God sent us here for Mukti (liberation). this guy is trapped in Mukta's charm." Everyone burst into laughter, and I shot Sandy an annoyed look.

To be continued ......

www.ingramcontent.com/pod-product-compliance
Lightning Source LLC
La Vergne TN
LVHW090049160826
845672LV00015B/1609

* 9 7 9 8 8 9 1 3 3 5 9 9 8 *